Why was he so attracted to her when she wasn't his usual type?

She wasn't wearing any makeup and her hair was tousled. She had circles under her eyes from lack of sleep and was dressed in a baggy sweater and old jeans.

But still he wanted her more than he'd ever wanted any woman. All he could think about was the tight, lithe body underneath her clothes and the way she had responded with such fire and heat in his arms three months ago.

Whenever he tried to concentrate at work, all he could think about was how different things could have been between him and Katie…if he'd known who she really was on that incredible night they'd shared.

Peter could think of at least a dozen ways to make love to her in every corner of this sprawling ranch house. The possibilities were limited only by his imagination and his stamina, and when it came to Katie Crosby, he had a feeling he would have more than enough of both to go around.

Maybe being snowbound together would work out in his favor, after all….

RaeANNE THAYNE

finds inspiration in the beautiful Northern Utah mountains where she lives with her husband and three children. Writing about a blizzard for *Intimate Surrender* reminded her how much she hates snow, but with two avid skiers in the family she has learned to endure. She loved working with all of the wonderful authors involved in the LOGAN'S LEGACY project, especially as many of them are her own favorite authors to read. She also discovered several new favorites. RaeAnne's books have won numerous honors, including a RITA® Award nomination from Romance Writers of America and a *Romantic Times* Reviewer's Choice nomination. She loves to hear from readers and can be reached through her Web site at www.raeannethayne.com or at P.O. Box 6682 North Logan, UT 84341.

LOGAN'S LEGACY

INTIMATE SURRENDER
RaeAnne Thayne

Silhouette Books

Published by Silhouette Books
America's Publisher of Contemporary Romance

Special thanks and acknowledgment are given
to RaeAnne Thayne for her contribution
to the LOGAN'S LEGACY series.

 SILHOUETTE BOOKS

ISBN 0-373-61391-1

INTIMATE SURRENDER

Be a part of

$\mathscr{L}$OGAN'S $\mathscr{L}$EGACY

*Because birthright has its privileges
and family ties run deep.*

**Two rivals share a passionate night together.
Would their love end a thirty-year-old family
feud?**

Katie Crosby: After a glorious makeover, she
was the belle of the ball. She even shared a kiss
with her enemy Peter Logan, which resulted in
a steamy night of lovemaking. Now in hiding from
the tabloids, Katie realized she had fallen in love.

Peter Logan: He was Mr. All-Work-And-No-Play
until his night with Katie. But she'd disappeared and
he had to find her. With luck and a well-timed
blizzard, he was in Katie's arms again…and ready
to make her a lifetime proposition!

The Janitor: Charlie Prescott had demons he kept
under wraps. And no one in the clinic had any idea
just how invested he was in the black-market baby
ring. Would the truth come out?

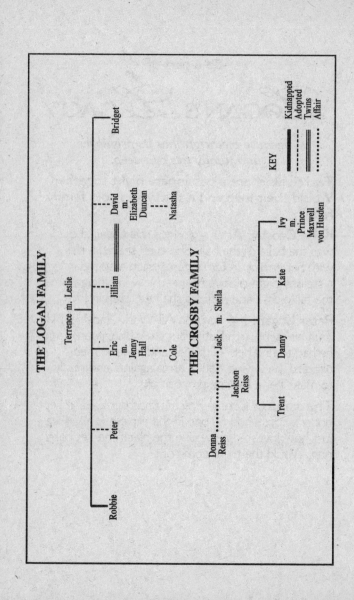

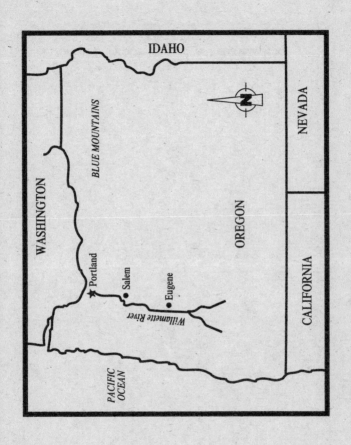

To Linda Kruger,
for unwavering support and encouragement.

One

"We shouldn't go. It's not right to leave you here alone. Not with a storm coming on."

Margie Taylor's sturdy features creased with worry, and her weathered, capable hand fretted with the handle of her suitcase. With his typical stoicism, her husband, Clint, took it from her and stowed it behind the seat in their king-cab Ford pickup.

Katie Crosby managed a patient smile, just as if she and Margie hadn't just spent the last three hours circling this same argument more times than a green-broke horse at the end of a lead line. "Don't be silly," she said. "I'll be just fine. I can take care of myself for a few days and you said you'd made arrangements for Darwin Simmons to come over from the Bar S to feed and water the stock. I don't foresee any problems."

"Still, I don't feel good about leaving you. You know we always try to be here when one of the family comes to Sweetwater."

"I know how seriously you and Clint take your responsibilities as caretakers of the ranch. You do a wonderful job here but you are certainly entitled to a private life, too."

Margie looked unconvinced and Katie squeezed her hand. "Your daughter needs you. It's her first baby and she's probably scared to death and needs her mother."

The bitter irony of her words didn't escape her, but Katie ignored the sudden pang in her chest. "You have to go to Idaho Falls," she went on. "I would feel just horrible if you missed seeing your new grandchild enter the world because of me."

"Weatherman says that storm is supposed to be a real doozy," Clint spoke up.

"Then you'd better hurry and get on your way so you aren't caught in it. I'll be fine, I promise."

"But what if you're stranded out here by yourself?" Margie asked, her forehead furrowed with worry.

"I won't mind, I promise. I came out from Portland looking for a little peace and quiet. I have plenty of books to read and the kitchen is fully stocked. I don't need anything else. As long as Darwin can take care of the stock, I'll be cozy and warm and snug as can be in the ranch house."

"I just don't feel right about this."

"Don't give me another thought. Just focus on Carly and that new grandbaby of yours."

Between her and Clint, they finally managed to herd Margie into the passenger seat of the truck, though she still looked worried.

Before they drove away, Clint rolled down the window. "If the power goes out, you'll have to start up the generator," he said gruffly. "Instructions are on the wall next to it."

"I'll be fine," she said for what seemed like the hundredth time. Through the open window she kissed him on the cheek, enjoying his blush. "Give the little darling a kiss for me, all right? Be safe."

He finally put the truck in gear and the four-wheel drive tires spit gravel as he headed down the long drive. Katie stood and watched them go while an unusually harsh wind for early March dug icy knuckles into her ribs inside her open canvas ranch coat. Despite her fleece hat, her head was freezing.

She should be used to this half-naked feeling after nearly three months without the heavy mane of hair she had always worn, but she still felt exposed with her new short, wispy hairstyle.

A few fluttery snowflakes settled on her skin and the canvas of her coat with deceptive gentleness. They might look lovely now, tiny swirling specks against the pale lavender twilight, but she knew a Wyoming winter storm could turn deadly with warp speed, even in March.

She had a feeling the weatherman was right about the storm. The air had a heavy, expectant quality to it, and thick dark clouds already concealed the tops of the mountains.

Katie filled her lungs with cold air that smelled of snow and lifted her face to the gossamer flakes.

She had always found peace out here and usually loved the view from the sprawling log-and-stone ranch house with its wide front porch and four gables along the steeply pitched roof. Even in winter, she could gaze for hours at the harsh and wild ring of snow-covered mountains that loomed over the ranch, the neat split-rail fences on either side of the driveway, the long row of bushy pine trees that formed a barrier from the endless Wyoming wind.

Try as she might, she knew she would find little comfort in the view this time. She was afraid peace would become a rare and elusive commodity in the coming months.

With a deep sigh, she reached a hand inside her coat and touched the tiny, barely noticeable bulge at her abdomen.

Just when, exactly, does a woman decide her life has spun completely and irrevocably out of her control? she wondered grimly.

Katie liked to think she was a fairly together kind

of person. Sure, she had her problems. Who didn't? So what if her best friend Carrie compared her to a hermit crab with agoraphobia and her mother still thought she was a fat, homely thirteen-year-old with bad vision and a serious addiction to comfort food?

She might lack the grace and poise one might expect from an offspring of one of the Northwest's wealthiest families. But besides thick, gooey macaroni and cheese, Katie had always comforted herself with the immutable knowledge that she had something far more important than charm and beauty and a twenty-inch waist.

She was smart. Off-the-charts smart. She wasn't arrogant about it—it was just a fact of life, like her brown eyes, her streaky brown hair, the tiny heart-shaped mole just above her left eyebrow.

She might not have grace and poise, but she *had* graduated summa cum laude from Stanford and become the vice president of research and development of one of the most powerful computer companies in the world. She knew her brother Trent relied on her logic and judgment at Crosby Systems and used her often as a sounding board.

So how, she wondered now as she gazed at the charcoal clouds gathering force, did she find herself in this predicament? Pregnant and alone and deep in the grip of a major panic attack?

Two days ago when her OB had confirmed the suspicion she hadn't even dared admit to herself, that panic had virtually paralyzed her. She had told herself the queasiness that had plagued her for several weeks must be some kind of lingering bug, had attributed her missed periods to stress and fatigue.

Hoping she only needed time away from the high stress of her life, she had come to the ranch, her own personal refuge, to recharge her batteries. After several weeks of telecommuting, the fatigue and the nausea hadn't abated. She returned to Portland for a meeting she couldn't miss and finally decided to see her doctor, who delivered the stunning news.

She had somehow driven in a numb haze to her condo and had sat in her living room all night long with the curtains drawn and the lights off.

The next morning she could think of nothing but returning to this haven where she had always felt such safety and solace. Maybe the clean mountain air would help her figure out how to cope with the atomic bomb that had just detonated in her neatly ordered life.

In the last few days, she'd had more time to get used to the idea that she was going to be a mother in a little over six months but she still didn't have the first idea how to chart out the rest of her life. She had always been one for blueprints and goals and lists, even as a little girl. So how was she supposed to pencil in an unplanned pregnancy at age twenty-eight, especially when her child's father didn't even know her real name?

She meant what she said to Margie. She was almost glad they had planned to leave for the birth of their new grandchild. As much as she loved the ranch caretakers, they tended to hover over her. Right now she desperately needed solitude—time to ponder and meditate and somehow shape an entirely new life plan for herself, one that included the tiny baby growing inside her.

One that certainly didn't include the child's father, no matter how much she might wish things could be different.

Kate shook off the foolish thought. A smart woman could never believe she and her baby's father would ever have more than the one incredible night they had shared.

An hour later she had just added another log to the fire in the massive river-rock fireplace of the great room and was settling onto the comfy couch with a mug of hot cocoa and a book she knew she wouldn't be able to concentrate on when she heard the bass rumble of a vehicle approaching.

What had Margie and Clint forgotten? she wondered. At this rate, they would find themselves stuck out here in the middle of the approaching blizzard.

A blast of cold air hit her as soon as she hurried to open the door for them. She shivered and saw that in the short time since she had stood in the driveway watching them leave, a half-inch of snow had fallen.

The sun had slid behind the mountains and in the pale lavender twilight, she could make out a late-model SUV approaching the house.

Not Clint and Margie, then. Odd. They hadn't mentioned they were expecting anyone.

From the entryway, she watched a man climb out of the vehicle and had an impression of lean, muscular strength. She saw only dark wavy hair and a leather aviator jacket, then he turned to face her and the stoneware mug slipped from her clumsy fingers.

She reached for it just in time to keep the whole thing from gushing out all over the wood floor. Hot cocoa splashed her jeans but she barely registered it. She could focus on only one horrifying realization.

He had found her!

She couldn't seem to draw enough breath into her lungs as Peter Logan slammed the door to the SUV and stalked up the porch stairs. The blood rushed away from her oxygen-starved brain and she swayed, fighting a panicked urge to slam the door and shove the heavy hall table across it as a barricade against his anger. It took every ounce of concentration to keep her hands clenched tightly at her sides, not covering the tiny, barely there life growing inside her.

"Hello, Celeste." Her middle name came out more like a snarl.

Celeste. The name she'd used the night of the auction gala, when she'd kept her true identity a secret from him.

"Peter. Th-this is a surprise." She hated the stammer but couldn't seem to help it.

"I'll just bet it is."

She couldn't think what to say, could only stare at him as wild memories crowded through her mind of how that tight, angry mouth had once been tender and sensual, had once explored every inch of her skin.

"Are you going to stand there staring at me all night like I'm the Abominable Snowman come to call, or do you think you might condescend to let me inside?"

Did she have a choice? If she did, her vote would have been for locking him out on the porch rather than face a confrontation with him. But since she had a pretty good idea that a man like Peter Logan wouldn't let anything as inconsequential as a locked door keep him away, she had no choice but to surrender to the inevitable. She stepped aside.

"What are you doing here, Peter?"

"You mean how did I figure out who the hell you really were?"

Despite her best efforts at control, she shivered at the menace in his tone. "That, too."

"Don't you read the papers, sweetheart?"

She stared at him blankly. Across the vast room, she was oddly aware of a log breaking apart in the fireplace with a hiss and crackle. After a moment he yanked a folded newspaper from the inside pocket of his snow-flecked leather jacket and slapped it down on the narrow hall table next to her.

She eyed it like he'd just let loose a wolverine in the Sweetwater great room. Warily, her pulse skipping with sudden trepidation, Katie picked up the newspaper. It was a copy of the society page of *Portland Weekly,* the independent tabloid that delighted in poking fun at the city's movers and shakers.

Her gaze went to the photo first and her already queasy stomach dipped. It was a photo of her and the man now standing before her, both of them in elegant evening wear. Her back—bared in a glittery emerald-colored designer gown she'd borrowed from her best friend—was to the camera, but anybody who saw the picture could clearly identify Peter Logan—and could see the two of them were locked in a passionate embrace.

She had seen it before. The newspaper had run the photo months ago as part of a feature spread of a bachelor auction and charity benefit for Children's Connection, a Portland adoption agency and fertility clinic. The caption had said only something about Peter being photographed in a hot kiss with a mystery woman. When they ran it the first time, she had seen it and thanked her very lucky stars that she hadn't been recognizable.

Apparently someone had figured it out. The headline above this photo read "Mystery Solved: Crosby,

Logan scions put aside famous feud long enough
for kiss."

Oh, no. She drew in a shaky breath. This was bad.
Seriously bad. She read on.

> "We first brought you the juicy tidbit a few
> months ago that Logan Corporation CEO and
> oh-so-sexy bachelor Peter Logan was caught in
> a very heated embrace with a mysterious glam-
> our-gal during a chi-chi gala for Children's
> Connection, a cause the Logan family notably
> supports. The two of them disappeared together
> soon after.
>
> At the time. Logan pointedly refused to an-
> swer questions about the object of his affec-
> tions, but after some digging, *Portland Weekly*
> has since learned his snuggle-honey was none
> other than Katherine Crosby. That's right, of
> *those* Crosbys—Logan rivals on and off the
> corporate battlefield.
>
> Does their embrace signal an end to the fa-
> mous feud? Are Portland's own versions of the
> Hatfield and McCoy clans really ready to kiss
> and make up?
>
> Apparently at least two of them are.
>
> Neither Logan nor Ms. Crosby were avail-
> able for comment but we'll bring you more
> about this exciting development as soon as we
> find out more."

Her already queasy stomach dipped. Her mother was bound to hear about this; Katie had no doubt whatsoever about that. And when she did, Katie knew Sheila Crosby would rage and carry on for days, accusing her of everything from disloyalty to outright treason.

Just thinking about the inevitable scene made her shoulders sag with the exhaustion that never seemed far away these days.

"Nothing to say?" Peter finally asked when her silence dragged on.

"I've never been called a glamour-gal before. I don't believe it's as gratifying as I would have imagined."

His sculpted features darkened. "I dislike being made a fool of, Katherine."

"Kate," she murmured, regretting the glibness she tended to turn to during times of high stress. "Nearly everyone calls me Katie or Kate."

"Really, Celeste?" He asked in that same biting tone.

Oh, Katie. What a mess you're in, she thought. Pregnant with this man's baby, this overwhelming, powerful, *gorgeous* man who despised her and her family. If he hated her now, how would he react if he ever discovered the tiny secret she carried inside her?

The fragile threads of control seemed to slip a few more notches, but she flailed for them valiantly and faced him with what she hoped was cool aplomb.

Without waiting for the invitation she wasn't sure she could issue, he yanked off his jacket and tossed it over the rack of entwined elk antlers in the hallway then claimed one of the plump armchairs near the fire. She really had no choice but to follow him and perched on the edge of the sofa, trying not to let him see her nervousness.

"Okay, let's hear it. What's your game?"

"Game?"

"What are you playing at? What were you trying to achieve by your little masquerade?"

Of course he would want explanations from her, some justification for her deception. How could she possibly find the words for something she didn't even understand herself?

"Why didn't you tell me who you were?"

"I don't know that I have a good answer to that."

"Try." His voice was silk-sheathed steel.

She scrambled for some kind of explanation and finally came up with something she hoped sounded reasonable. It was part of the truth, just not all of it. "Katie Crosby is a fairly boring person," she said after a long moment. "All she ever thinks about is work. I suppose it was exciting being someone else for a few hours. Someone glamorous and adventurous and…and desirable. I got carried away by the magic of the evening. Then, after we…kissed, I was afraid to tell you who I was. I knew you would be angry and it just seemed easier all around not to say anything."

* * *

Peter studied her. She chewed her bottom lip after she finished speaking, waiting for him to respond. He wondered how in the hell a woman could appear so sweet and innocent on the outside while inside she was nothing but a deceptive little snake.

He had never been so furious. It was taking every ounce of willpower he possessed not to rage and yell and throw a table or two through that huge wall of windows.

His blood should have had time to cool in the twenty-four hours since his assistant had warily shown him that damn newspaper and he'd finally learned the identity of the mystery lover who had obsessed him for months. It had taken him most of that time to use all his connections and finally run her to ground here at this Wyoming ranch in the middle of nowhere, another hour to have his plane readied and two more in the air between here and Portland.

The whole time he'd been behind the controls of his Gulfstream III, he had waited for his anger to fade, for the familiar cool reserve the world expected of him to take over. But throughout the flight, as now, his skin had been hot and itchy as this fury seethed through him.

This woman—this slender, delicate-looking woman with her short hair and big eyes, who looked like a teenager in stocking feet and faded jeans—had made a complete fool out of him. Every word out of her lush little lips had been a lie.

When he thought about how he had obsessed over her in the three months since she blew through his life, the energy he had wasted looking for her, he could barely think past his rage and self-disgust.

A Crosby.

Just the name left a sour taste in his mouth. What an idiot he had been to throw away years of family loyalty, of complete dedication to the Logan name and everything it stood for, all for a pretty face.

All right, more than pretty, he admitted. Even now, when she wore no makeup to set off those sculpted cheekbones and full lips and when she had dark circles under her eyes and her features were pale, his body instinctively reacted to her.

He wanted her, even knowing who she was, and the discovery infuriated him even more.

"This is about the super router we're developing, isn't it?" he asked.

She was a hell of an actress, he'd give her that much. If he didn't know better, he would almost believe that shock on her face was genuine. "What do you mean?" she asked.

"You went through my desk while I was asleep. Don't try to deny it. Find out anything interesting about the project?"

Color flared high on those cheekbones. "I don't know what you're talking about."

"Right. Now you're going to tell me you don't have any idea Logan is close to revolutionizing computer networking with our nano-peripheral-interface-router. And of course Crosby Systems, which coincidentally just released its own router-controller software, would have absolutely no interest in stealing the technology that would create the fastest networking system in the world. Come on, Crosby. You really think I'm dumb enough to fall for your lies twice?"

She gaped at him. "You think I was spying on you that night? That I was some kind of—of corporate Mata Hari, out for a little industrial espionage after I screw you into oblivion?"

"At this point, sweetheart, I wouldn't put anything past you."

"Because I'm a Crosby, right?"

That wounded belligerence in her voice grated down his spine like metal on metal. "Not *only* because you're a Crosby. Because you're also a lying, deceitful little—" He bit off the derogatory word just in time.

He was such an idiot. He hated to think about how his family would react to his abysmal lapse in judgment when they learned he'd been willing to risk the company's entire future for a roll in the sack. He had a feeling he would be lucky if his name was still on the door of the CEO's office at Logan. Hell, he'd be lucky if they even let him keep the name he'd been given as a six-year-old.

He never forgot how much he owed Terrence

and Leslie Logan, how very blessed he had been to be adopted into their family two years after their own son had been kidnapped. If they hadn't rescued him from the Children's Connection orphanage, he hated thinking where he might have ended up. On the streets like his mother, probably, or in prison.

He owed them everything. His heart, his blood, his *soul*. When they read that damn tabloid article, he could just picture the disappointment in Terrence's eyes, the hurt in Leslie's. The knot in his stomach kinked a little tighter.

No. He had worked too hard for too long proving to his parents he was capable of running the Fortune 500 company they had built from the ground up. He refused to let a Crosby ruin everything, especially not this particular Crosby.

"Don't you think you're being a little paranoid, Peter?" she said now. "I never touched your desk."

Against his will, he had a vivid memory of her naked and flushed the second or third time they made love, her luscious skin glowing with perspiration and the soft little noises of arousal she made as he took her against the nearest surface, which at the time just happened to be the top of his antique walnut desk.

Throughout that incredible night of passion, there had scarcely been a corner of his loft they'd missed in their hunger for each other.

He raised an eyebrow but said nothing. He knew

the instant her own memory clicked in. A rosy blush spilled over her cheeks and she dropped her gaze.

"Well, besides that time," she mumbled, looking so charmingly disconcerted he wondered how she could possibly be so deceitful.

"I've tried to think about what I might have had lying around about our NPIR project but I'm coming up empty. Why don't you refresh my memory? What did you find?"

"Nothing! I wasn't thinking about NPIRs or anything else computer related. I didn't go anywhere near your stupid desk, except that time with…you."

"Yet the note you left was written on my own personal stationery, which I just happen to keep in the top drawer of that stupid desk."

She stared at him for a long moment, then she drew a deep breath. When she spoke, her voice sounded weary. "What do you want, Peter? Why follow me out here to the middle of nowhere? You could have yelled at me over the phone."

He refused to let himself be sidetracked by how fragile she suddenly looked. "I want some answers. What did you learn about our project?"

"I didn't learn anything! I told you that. I never even gave work a thought that night. If you'll remember, you didn't give me time to think about much of anything but you."

They stared at each other for a moment and he remembered again the wild passion they had shared.

Or at least he thought they'd shared it. Had it all been feigned on her part? All those long kisses, her sighs and moans, the way she acted as if she couldn't seem to get enough of him?

That was the part that he was finding most difficult to accept, he finally admitted to himself. He had been enthralled with her, completely entranced. He had wanted her with a fierce hunger unlike anything he'd ever known before.

While she had been as cold-blooded and calculating as an asp.

"Did your brother tell you to sleep with me?" he asked.

With a swift intake of breath, she stared at him, her brown eyes huge in her pale face. In any other woman, he might have almost believed she looked hurt. But he obviously couldn't trust anything his instincts told him about Katherine Crosby.

"That's insulting to Trent and to me. I shouldn't even justify it with a response but I will tell you that he knows nothing about this, about the two of us and that night. If he did, he would be livid."

Peter slapped the folded tabloid at her. "Hate to be the one to break it to you, sweetheart, but there's not a person in Portland who doesn't know by now."

She gazed at the paper for a moment, nibbling her lip again. "Okay so everyone might know we kissed. As for the rest of it, no one else has to know anything about that. We were both carried away by the champagne and the night and the whole thing. Matters never should have gone so far. We should both just forget it ever happened."

"You'd like that, wouldn't you?"

"Oh, you have no idea," she murmured.

At her words, another wave of anger washed over him. The intensity of it had him jumping to his feet and stalking to the fireplace. He hated that she could just dismiss the night they had spent together. *Forget it ever happened.* Right. As if he could just forget the most erotic night of his life.

He turned back to her. "A smart man never forgets his mistakes. And, sweetheart, this was one hell of a mistake."

"For both of us."

"The difference is, you knew exactly what you were doing—and who you were doing it with."

"That's right. I set out to seduce you from the moment I walked into that ballroom. It was a brilliant strategy, wouldn't you say? All I had to do was convince you to take me home with you, make love all night until you fell asleep, then comb through your office on the chance—slim to none though it was—that I might find some tiny snippet of information in your loft about your super-router that we could use at Crosby Systems. Right. You caught me. That's me, Katie Crosby, corporate spy. Trent sends his little sister out to sleep with all his business rivals."

"I wouldn't put anything past the Crosbys."

Something flashed in her dark eyes, something that looked like anger and hurt and maybe even a little sorrow. "Okay, that's enough," she snapped. "I would like you to leave now. I'm sure you don't want to spend another moment in the belly of the beast."

She rose as if to show him out but as soon as she stood, what little color remaining on her face drained out like wine spilling from a tipped glass and she swayed. Peter reached out instinctively to keep her from toppling over, then helped her back onto the couch.

"What's wrong? Are you ill?"

Her chin lifted. "What do you care?"

"I don't," he snapped. "Maybe I just happen to be fond of these particular boots and don't want you yakking all over them."

She glared at him. "Your precious boots are safe. I'm not going to *yak,* as you so charmingly put it. I stood up a little too soon but I'm perfectly fine now."

He only had to take one look at her to know she was lying, but then why should that surprise him? The woman wouldn't know the truth if it jumped up and bit her in the behind. With hollow eyes, her skin three shades past white and her mouth pinched like a shriveled apple left in the bottom of the bushel, she sat there and expected him to believe everything was fine.

"I didn't see signs of anybody else when I arrived. Who else is out here with you?"

She paused as if she didn't want to answer him,

then she finally shrugged. "Usually the ranch foreman and his wife live in quarters at the rear of the
house, but they're away for a few days."

"You're alone?"

"Not if you count two dogs, six barn cats, a dozen
horses and two hundred head of cattle."

He studied her pale features again, suddenly chagrined at himself for bursting in on her, guns blazing. She might be a lying Crosby but she didn't look
well at all.

Crosby or not, he didn't like the idea of her being
out here alone. A thousand things could happen to an
ill woman on her own at an isolated Wyoming ranch,
especially with the storm percolating out there.

"If you're done yelling at me, I really would like
you to leave now." Somehow she managed to inject
regal condescension into her words, even with her
pale features.

"I really think I should stay," he found himself
saying.

Her eyes widened and he didn't miss the way her
hand clenched over her stomach, as if just the idea
of spending another moment with him was enough
to make her insides churn.

"No. No, you shouldn't. The weather report said
a nasty storm is heading this way. You'll want to fly
back to Portland before it hits."

"It's already here. Can't you hear that wind? The
reports I heard before I landed said this area was due

for at least two feet of snow. I won't be flying any-where tonight."

"If you heard the storm reports before you left, why fly out here in such a rush? Acting on a whim like that hardly seems like typical behavior for the cold, ruthless CEO of Logan Corporation."

Nothing he had done since he'd seen her in that hotel ballroom had been typical behavior for him. He had seen the reports of an approaching storm in this area before he left Portland, but not even flying into the eye of a hurricane would have kept him grounded.

He had known he was foolish to leave but he had been so angry he hadn't cared about anything but running her to ground, after three long months of searching.

"It doesn't matter why I left," he answered. "I'm not going anywhere."

"I'm not in the mood for your macho posturing, Peter. I don't want or need you here."

"Fickle little thing, aren't you? Three months ago, you certainly wanted me around. If my memory serves—and believe me, it does—you couldn't get enough."

She glared at him, though he saw yet another blush heat those cheeks. "Which am I? Ruthless cor-porate spy or sex-crazed nymphomaniac?"

"Good question. One I would certainly like to know the answer to myself."

Before she could give voice to the heated response

he could see brewing, a powerful gust of wind rattled the windowpanes and moaned under the eaves of the log ranch house.

The two lamps burning in the room flickered in unison then went out, pitching the room into darkness lit only by the fire's glow.

Two

"That settles it. I'm not going anywhere."

Even though the only light in the room came from the snapping flames in the fireplace, Katie could see the determination in Peter's eyes and she wanted to weep. Just when she thought she had hit absolute rock bottom in her life, somehow she managed to cartwheel down another few feet.

She suddenly wanted nothing in the world more than to curl up on that couch in front of the fireplace, wrap herself in her grandmother's wedding-ring quilt and sob.

What had she done to deserve this? Okay, maybe she hadn't been exactly forthcoming to Peter Logan three months earlier. In retrospect, she knew she should have told him her real name the moment he struck up a conversation with her, at the first sign of flirtation.

She wasn't sure why she had kept that important little detail to herself—maybe because she had been so shocked that the gorgeous and sought-after Peter Logan could actually be flirting with someone like her—boring, quiet Katie Crosby.

Who could blame any woman for being caught up in the magic of the evening? With a glamorous make-over, a new hairstyle, the designer clothes, she had *felt* like someone else. A stranger alluring enough to catch the interest of one of Portland's most wanted bachelors.

The champagne she had overindulged in hadn't helped any. She hadn't been thinking with a clear head but she did know she hadn't wanted the night to end. She also knew that the moment Peter found out her last name that flattering desire in his eyes would have changed to contempt and coldness faster than she could blink.

Okay, so she had perpetuated a tiny deception on the man by keeping her identity concealed. Was that really such a hideous crime that someone felt the need to take her calm, organized world and shake the dickens out of it as if she was stuck in some night-marish live snow globe?

She thought things were bleak before when she

was just pregnant and alone. Now she had the delightful added bonus of facing the reality that she was pregnant and alone and heartily despised by her baby's father.

The real hell of it was, seeing him again like this only served to remind her vividly of the heat and astonishing wonder of that night. Of kissing his hard mouth and touching those muscles underneath his clothes and burning only for him.

He hated her, she knew he did, but still she couldn't control the way her insides trembled and sighed just seeing the firelight wash across those gorgeous, masculine features.

"Looks like we're in for a long night," he said abruptly and rose to his feet. "While you round up a flashlight and some candles, I'll go bring in some extra firewood."

Of course he would take charge, she thought. As Logan Corporation CEO, he was no doubt used to giving orders and having his minions obey without question. She should have been offended by his whole master-and-commander routine but she had to admit a tiny part of her wanted to let him throw his weight around a little, to let someone else carry the burdens of her worries for a while.

She sternly squashed the tempting impulse, ashamed of her weakness for even entertaining it for a second. "You don't need to do that. Clint loaded several days worth of wood on the back porch for me before he left. There's also a gas-fired generator out back that will juice up the appliances until the power kicks back on."

"You act as if you've been through this before."

"A few times. The power can be unreliable at best out here, especially during winter storms. I've had enough experience with outages that I should be perfectly fine. Believe me, you can head into town for the night with a completely clear conscience."

She might as well have been talking to the river rocks on the fireplace. His only answer was a raised eyebrow and a challenging stare.

Katie sighed. It was worth a try. The idea of spending even one night in such close quarters with Peter Logan was enough to send her into major panic mode.

He was staying, though, and she realized grimly that no amount of arguing would change his mind. The same man who had the kindness as an eighteen-year-old college student to rescue a fat, awkward adolescent from the ugliness of her peers more than a decade earlier would never leave a woman alone out here in the middle of a blizzard.

"I don't suppose you know anything about generators, do you?" she asked. "I've seen Clint start it but never done it myself."

"Between the two of us, we should be able to figure it out, don't you think?"

Relieved that he seemed willing to put aside his animosity, even temporarily, she nodded. "Sure."

He cocked his head. "Are you sure you're up to it? You're still looking a little green around the edges. Maybe you should just take it easy and lie down here by the fire. I'm sure I can handle starting up a generator on my own."

She refused to let him see how very much she would like to do exactly that, just curl up on this couch and let him handle everything. Trying her best to conceal the greasy nausea writhing around in her stomach, she mustered a small smile.

"Don't worry about me." Using the fire's glow for illumination, she crossed the vast room to the hall storage closet. On the shelf near the door, just where she expected it, she found a large battery-powered lantern Clint and Margie kept available for exactly these kinds of emergencies. Wouldn't she love it if the engineers on her R & D team were half as efficient as the Sweetwater caretakers? she thought.

"This should help," she said to Peter. She led the way toward the utility porch off the kitchen. It seemed as if in just the few moments since the power had gone out, the temperature in the rooms away from the fireplace had dropped significantly. The Mexican tile floor in the kitchen was freezing, even through her thick wool socks.

All she could see outside the greenhouse window above the sink was thick blackness, but she could hear snow hurling against the logs and the wind moaning under the eaves.

It sounded lonely, mournful, and she shivered despite the sweater Ivy had sent her for Christmas from her new husband's country of Lantanya, where Max was king.

The lantern gave off enough light that Peter must have seen her reaction. "Everything okay? Do you need to sit down?"

She knew the concern in his voice was just the courtesy he would show anyone but she couldn't help being warmed by it. She had a feeling he wouldn't be so solicitous if he knew the secret she carried under that sweater, though.

"No. The cold just took me by surprise, that's all. The generator is this way."

With the lantern held out in front of her, she carefully navigated through the mudroom to the utility porch that housed the home's utilities—the furnace, water heater and the backup generator. The large room was vented with outside air for safety reasons and Katie found it even colder here than in the kitchen, so cold she could see her breath in the dim light she held in her hand.

"Any idea where to start?" Peter asked.

"Clint told me he left instructions." She held the lantern up higher and scanned the room.

"This what you were looking for?" Peter asked, plucking a clipboard from a nail near the generator. He handed it to her and she saw several laminated cards secured neatly to it.

"I'll say this for the man—he doesn't have much to say but he's an absolute genius at organization." Katie leafed through the cards until she found guidelines for the gas-fired generator, beneath a page detailing how to relight the pilot on the furnace and one for checking the heating oil level on the outside tank.

"Here we go." She studied the instructions, smiling a little at Clint's meticulousness. "This doesn't look bad."

She reached to replace the clipboard on the nail but misjudged the distance in the dim light and stumbled a little against the wall. The back of her hand scraped across the nail, hard enough to break the skin, and Katie couldn't contain a quick intake of breath.

"What's wrong?"

It was silly, she knew, but she suddenly didn't want Peter to know she was the world's biggest klutz. She might have been blessed with brains by some genetic quirk, but she had definitely been passed over when it came to grace and poise.

She had always been the most accident-prone of her siblings. If there was one thing worse than being fat and ugly in a family of beautiful people, it was being fat and ugly and clumsy.

Peter already thought she had some deadly disease. He didn't need to know about this.

"Um, nothing," she murmured, tucking her hand against her side. "I'm fine."

"You're lying." He sounded more resigned than

angry, as if he expected nothing else. "You might as well tell me what happened."

Her hand throbbed wickedly and she could feel blood beginning to drip from it. She wouldn't be able to hide it from him for long and she suddenly felt foolish for trying. "Just a scratch. It's nothing."

"Let me see."

She recognized the CEO in his voice, that unmistakable note of command. Her father had it and now Trent shared it in spades. She had spent her entire life surrounded by powerful men, she suddenly realized. With all that experience, why wasn't she better at dealing with them?

With a weary sigh, she thrust out her hand. Peter took the lantern from her and set it on top of the furnace, then gripped her hand and tugged it under the circle of light.

"It doesn't look very deep," he decided after studying it for a few moments.

"I told you it was just a scratch."

"Still, you'll need to put something on it."

"Can it wait until we're finished here, Dr. Logan?"

"I hope your tetanus shot is up to date. That nail looked a little rusty."

Someone with her inherent klutziness would be foolish not to keep current with her shots. Her last tetanus booster had been the previous summer after an unfortunate encounter with a conch shell on her brother Danny's Hawaii retreat.

"Don't worry, you're not going to be trapped in the middle of a blizzard with someone suffering from lockjaw."

"Well, at least I've got that much going for me. I guess things really could be worse."

His dry tone surprised a laugh from her. Not much of one, she had to admit, but a laugh nonetheless.

He smiled in automatic response, his teeth gleaming in the artificial light. They stood close together under the pool of light spilling from the lantern. He still held her hand, and his fingers were warm and hard on her skin.

His gaze met hers for a moment and suddenly she could think of nothing except their night together, how they had laughed at nothing and kissed and laughed some more.

Everything inside her seemed to clench at the memory, a long, slow tightening of muscle and nerves. She saw something kindle in his eyes, something hot and wild and dangerous.

Before she realized it, she swayed a little toward him, then caught herself just in time. Horrified at her response, she wrenched her hand out of his grasp and stepped back so quickly she nearly stumbled again.

"We'd better get this thing fired up."

For a moment, he only stared at her with an odd look in his dark eyes—a combination of awareness and a baffled sort of anger. "Right," he finally muttered. "The wind sounds like it's kicking up a notch."

To her vast relief, he turned his attention to the generator. It was a little trickier than Clint's instructions had led her to believe, but soon they had it going and switched the power current over to the generator.

Despite the tension simmering through the room and the pain still throbbing from her finger, she felt like Benjamin Franklin with his kite and his key when the lights flickered back on.

She grinned. "Bingo."

He gazed at her for a charged moment, that strange expression in his eyes again. She waited for him to say something but he continued to watch her, as if he couldn't quite figure her out.

She cleared her throat. "Would you like something to eat? Margie left a pot of beef stew on the stove for me that's probably still hot and she made fresh rolls this morning. It's probably not what you're used to, but she's a wonderful cook."

"Let's take care of that cut of yours first."

She absolutely did not want him touching her again, not when she couldn't stop remembering how his body had felt inside her, how his mouth had explored her skin.

"I've got it. You could add another log to the fire, though, and turn off any lights and nonessential electronics throughout the house. We'll need to conserve what generator power we have. Here, take the lantern. I've got another one in my bedroom."

He nodded and held out his hand. Their fingers brushed as they exchanged the light, and tiny sparks jumped between them. Just static electricity, she told herself.

They returned to the kitchen together, then split up as she headed for her bedroom suite. She left the overhead light on long enough to locate another battery-powered emergency lantern in her closet, switched it off and carried the lantern to the bathroom to get first-aid supplies.

While she rummaged through the medicine cabinet for a bandage and antibiotic ointment and washed the blood off her hand, she caught sight of her reflection in the mirror above the sink. She looked horrendous. Her hair was spiky and windblown from her time outside earlier and she hadn't bothered with makeup. Her eyes looked unnaturally huge in her pale face and her mouth had a pinched, sickly look to it.

No wonder Peter looked at her like he couldn't quite believe Katie Crosby and the glamorous Celeste could be the same person.

She could scarcely believe it herself. She had been playing a part that night, a thrilling masquerade. Stuck alone here with her, Peter would see the real her. The boring, sensible Kate who wore long underwear and read dry technical manuals and who would never dream of going home with a handsome man and making love all night long.

Well, okay, she dreamed about it, she admitted to herself with a long, honest look in the mirror. She dreamed about it every night and remembered in exquisitely painful detail how she had come alive for the first time in her life that night.

Perhaps it was best that he see her for the person she really was. Not glamorous, not glitzy. Just Katie. That night she had been Cinderella at the ball, dressed up in borrowed finery. It had been wonderful and magical dancing the night away with Prince Charming, but midnight had come and gone. There would be no glass slipper for her—but she had been left with a magical, wondrous gift.

She touched her abdomen. Could she keep the baby a secret from him in such close quarters? It was only for one night and then he would be gone again. She was only thirteen weeks along and wasn't really showing unless someone knew her well enough to recognize that the tiny swelling at her stomach hadn't been there a few weeks ago.

She would just have to make sure she stayed in baggy clothes so he wouldn't have that close a look.

The pesky morning sickness could be explained away by a lingering stomach bug, she hoped.

It would be a little tricky to pull it off, but what other choice did she have? She couldn't tell him. This was *her* baby. He might have unwittingly donated the sperm but that didn't make him a father. Bad enough that she deceived him by not telling him her name—she couldn't bind him forever to a Crosby because of a quirk of fate.

Besides, Peter Logan was not the father she wanted for her baby. He was far too much like her own father—completely consumed by his work. She knew what it was like to wait in vain for a few crumbs her busy, important father might scatter her way. She wouldn't do that to her own child. Better for her baby never to know a father than to suffer from inattention and indifference.

She could carry off the deception for one night, then they would go their separate ways and Peter would never have to know about the baby. She would invent an imaginary lover for the inevitable questions from her family and friends about her child's paternity—a man she had fallen hard for but who had been unattainable.

Not so very far from the truth, she thought grimly. In fact, too close for her own comfort.

With a weary sigh, she quickly brushed her hair and debated touching up her face with some of the makeup tricks Carrie Summers had shown her. In the end she decided against doing anything more than a quick brush of lipstick and a little blush on her cheeks so she didn't look so ghastly pale.

She returned to the gathering room to find that Peter had pulled a small table and two chairs near the fireplace and had set out two place settings. She nibbled her lip, fighting the urge to turn back around and hide out in her room for the rest of the night.

Dinner for two in a dimly lit room in front of a crackling fire looked entirely too romantic, too *intimate*.

He stood by one of the chairs waiting for her with a challenging kind of look in his eyes and she knew she couldn't be cowardly enough to run away. She squared her shoulders and sat down.

"I hope you don't mind me moving the furniture around a little," he said. "I figured this would be more comfortable than eating in a cold dining room."

"The dining room is rarely used anyway. When I stay here, I usually eat in the kitchen with the Taylors."

"Those are the caretakers?"

She nodded. "Their daughter is having her first baby. They've gone for moral support."

"I hope they made it through the storm."

"I'm sure they'll be fine. Clint's used to driving in this weather."

She returned to stirring her stew and the Herculean effort of swallowing the occasional bite.

"This is quite a place you've got here," Peter said. "Somehow I never would have figured the Crosbys to go for rustic and isolated."

The faint note of derision in his voice raised her hackles. She wasn't sure if it was aimed at her family or at the ranch, both of which she loved dearly. Either way she didn't like it. A sharp retort formed in her throat but she squashed it. In the interest of peace, she should probably do her best to avoid needless bickering.

"My father bought it as a retreat several years ago when it seemed like everybody was moving west."

Like many of Jack Crosby's actions, Sweetwater had been purchased to please one of his many girlfriends, then had been forgotten as soon as her father moved on to more nubile pastures. But she decided that was old family business she didn't particularly need to share with Peter Logan.

"Does your family spend much time here together?" he asked.

She tried to remember when the Crosbys had last done anything together.

"We all came out for Christmas once right after Jack bought it," she remembered. "Trent and Ivy have been out to ski occasionally. Sweetwater is only about an hour from the Jackson Hole ski resorts."

He broke a roll in half and liberally spread some of Margie's strawberry preserves on it. "Is that why you're here? To ski?"

She wasn't sure quite how to answer that. She certainly couldn't tell him she had escaped to Sweetwater first because she'd been ill and then because she had been desperately in need of a safe haven, a sanctuary where she could come to terms with her pregnancy and figure out how she was going to map out the rest of her life after this unexpected detour.

"I'm not much of a skier," she finally said.

She would have preferred to leave it at that but he pressed on. "So why are you here?"

Katie fought the urge to gnash her teeth at what was beginning to feel like an interrogation. "I like it here. Of all my siblings, I probably spend the most time here. This is where I come when I need to relax and recharge. I love the mountains, even in the winter. I like the solitude of it and the slow, easy pace. I guess I just needed a break from the rain."

"So you decided howling winds and three feet of snow would be more to your liking?"

"It doesn't snow all the time," she muttered. She frowned suddenly, remembering something that had been puzzling her since he arrived. "How did you know how to find me, anyway? Only a few people knew I was coming."

"You know, it's amazing. The truth can open all kinds of doors. Maybe you ought to try it sometime."

Before she could control it, her breath caught as the jab poked under her skin. She deserved it, she acknowledged, especially with the secret she still kept from him, the one she knew she could never tell him. Knowing his contempt was warranted didn't make it any easier to take.

"Who told you?"

"I phoned your office. Once I gave your assistant my name and told her I needed to speak with you on an urgent matter, she was eager to help. She said you were staying at the family ranch and gave me the number here. From there, it was easy to connect the phone number to a location."

She should have known. If Peter hadn't been there, Katie would have groaned and banged her head against the back of her chair a few times. She loved her sixty-year-old assistant dearly but Lila Fitzgerald had a romantic streak as wide as the Columbia Gorge. She read the *Weekly* faithfully and must have seen the picture of them together at the bachelor auction.

Katie could just guess at the wild speculation that must have been running amok through Lila's feverish imagination when Peter had called looking for her.

What kind of gossip was raging around the water coolers at Crosby Systems about her and Peter Logan because of that blasted picture? There were already some on her team who thought she didn't have the experience or the know-how to lead the R & D division. What would her co-workers think when they saw a picture of her consorting with the man many considered to be the enemy?

What would her family think?

She already knew Sheila would be livid. She could only be grateful her mother was in Europe and wouldn't be returning for several weeks. What about Trent and Ivy and Danny? They wouldn't care so much that Peter was a Logan, but they would worry whether he had hurt her. And when she turned up pregnant, she knew they would wonder at the timing. She just had to hope she could brazen it out.

"I'm still not sure why you went to all the trouble to come out here. If you had the number, why couldn't we have had this delightful little reunion over the phone?"

Peter didn't have a rational answer to that. He only knew that the moment he found out where she was, he'd known he would come after her. He'd used the excuse of finding out what she had learned about the super-router project, but the truth was he'd been consumed with the need to see her again, corporate spy or not.

He'd be damned before he told her that, though, and he opted to change the subject. "Are you going to eat this delicious stew or just push it around in the bowl?"

Color crept along her cheekbones but she still looked far too pale for him. "I'm not very hungry."

"Still feeling sick?"

Her gaze flashed to his, then back to the bowl of stew. "No. I'm fine."

He didn't want to worry about her. He wanted to wrap himself up in his well-deserved fury.

She had deceived him, had possibly stolen Logan secrets from him, jeopardizing a project that had been in the works for years. Maybe even jeopardizing his own future at Logan.

She was a *Crosby,* for hell's sake. That alone should have been enough to squash any softness he might be tempted to feel.

So why was he fighting the completely inappropriate urge to take care of her?

"Have you seen a doctor?" he asked abruptly.

That color spread until even her nose was pink. "It's just a—a bug. Nothing to worry about."

"Is it contagious?"

A corner of her lush mouth lifted at that, then settled back into solemn lines. "No. I can guarantee you won't catch this particular bug."

A particularly strong gust of wind rattled the big window, but the merry little fire put out plenty of heat.

Peter couldn't help wondering what they would be doing right now if circumstances had been different. If she wasn't ill, certainly, but also if he had never learned her true identity.

Two days ago he would have given everything he had to be right here with the woman who had haunted his dreams for three months. To be alone with Celeste in an isolated ranch house, snug and warm and enchanted, would have been a fantasy come true. They would have snuggled under a blanket and listened to the wind howl outside while they kissed and touched and made love a dozen times.

The reality of their situation was so far removed from that fantasy that he gave a humorless laugh.

"What?"

"Just wondering what your brother would say if he knew I was here," he improvised quickly.

"I'm old enough that I don't need to ask my brother's permission for much these days."

The depressing reality of their situation here made his voice sharper than he intended. "Do you bother to ask him which unwitting business rivals to seduce, or do you figure that out all on your own?"

He regretted the words and the end to their temporary détente as soon as they escaped, especially when he saw hurt flare in her brown eyes. Was the emotion real, he wondered, or was she just a damn good actress? Whatever the answer, he didn't like seeing her wounded.

Her chair scraped the wood floor and she pushed it back and rose, her expression now veiled. "I'm tired and I don't have the energy to trade barbs with you, so what do you say we call it a night?"

He opened his mouth to apologize for his cruelty then stopped himself just in time. He didn't have a damn thing to be sorry about. She was the one who had screwed him over.

"Sweetwater has six bedrooms suites," she went on. "Two on this floor and five upstairs. Each has clean linens and a wood stove or fireplace for warmth. I'm sure you're capable of starting your own fire, or you can sleep here on the couch if you would rather."

"Kate—" He wasn't sure what he was going to

say. *Not* an apology, damn it. She cut him off anyway before he could form any kind of coherent sentence.

"Good night, Peter," she murmured in a voice every bit as cold as that bitch of a wind, then she picked up her bowl with its untouched stew and carried it to the kitchen.

Three

After her grand exit, Katie knew she had no choice but to hide here in her bedroom for the rest of the night.

It was too early to sleep, only about eight-thirty or so. She was tired enough, certainly—she was always tired these days—but even if she could manage to close her eyes, she had no doubt her mind would continue its wild race. She had a whole assortment of books to read, but none of them grabbed her interest. Why bother when she knew she wouldn't be able to concentrate on it anyway?

Surrendering to the inevitable, she pulled the quilt up to her chin and gazed into the flames and let her mind replay the night of the Children's Connection bachelor auction, one small slice of time that had altered the course of her life forever.

Stand up straight and smile. If you feel beautiful, the world will see you that way. Her best friend Carrie's advice rang in her ears as Katie stood outside the ballroom at the Portland Hilton.

Trouble was, she didn't feel beautiful. The borrowed dress was gorgeous and she liked the wispy supershort new haircut Carrie's stylist had given her, but she couldn't help feeling like a fraud.

This was a crazy idea, thinking a new look would change who she was inside, would somehow instantly transform her into someone glamorous and desirable.

Inside she still felt fat and dowdy and shy.

She would have been content to stay forever in the background. But then she received an e-mail from Stacy Cartier, an old friend at boarding school, who happened to mention she'd heard through the grapevine that another of their classmates Angelina Larson had come back to Portland for a visit and would be attending with her husband, Steve—who just happened to be Katie's ex-fiancé.

She hadn't seen Steve in years, not since she threw his ring at his head after she overheard him at a party laughing and joking with one of his friends about the little cash cow he was marrying.

She *had* been forty pounds overweight but she

thought he loved her despite the extra weight and her propensity to feel most comfortable with her nose in a book. The realization that he was marrying her only for her family's money and connections had been a bitter betrayal she wasn't sure she had ever recovered from.

Though she never wanted to see him again, she was committed to attend this benefit auction. She had to be there but she suddenly couldn't bear to have Steve—or his wife, Angelina, who had tormented her mercilessly through their childhood—think she hadn't changed at all in the six years since she'd broken off the engagement. Hence the makeover, the haircut, the borrowed designer gown.

You look good, she reminded herself. *Better than you've ever looked in your life. Pretend you're beautiful and the world will see you that way.*

With one more deep breath for courage, Katie walked into the ballroom, festooned with magical twinkling lights and holiday greenery.

Maybe this was all for nothing, she thought. In this press of people, she likely wouldn't even run into Steve and Angelina. For a moment she stood there feeling lost, then she caught sight of her brother Trent talking to a group of people she didn't know.

She approached him, grabbing another flute of champagne from a passing waiter as she moved through the crowd. She stood behind him for a moment until he finished speaking, then tapped him on the shoulder when the group started to break up.

"What time do they start the bidding?" she asked. Trent was one of the bachelors up for bid; she had agreed to come in the first place only to give him moral support.

He turned at her words, a ready smile on his handsome features that slid away when he saw her. If she hadn't been so nervous about his reaction she would have laughed at the way his eyes widened and his jaw dropped.

"Katie?" he exclaimed. "What have you done to yourself? Where did you get that dress?"

The momentary delight she had taken at his stunned expression gave way to a flicker of annoyance. She hadn't expected him to put on his overprotective big brother act. Usually he reserved that for Ivy, since Katie seldom gave him any reason to worry.

"Carrie Summers. She has a whole closet full of designer clothes from her modeling days. Why? What's wrong with it?" she asked, when he continued to stare.

"Nothing, other than there isn't nearly enough of it." He cocked his head and took in all the changes she had made in the last few days. "You look incredible! You cut off all your hair. And where are your glasses? After all the years of Sheila's nagging, I can't believe you finally broke down and went for contacts."

Here's where things might get a little tricky, she thought. "I, um, had laser correction surgery earlier in the week. That's why I haven't been into the office. It was my Christmas present to myself."

Just as she feared, his commanding features tightened. "Surgery? You had *surgery* and you didn't bother to tell me? Why not? If you'd told me, I could have checked out the doctors and the facility, even researched the procedure. Hell, at the very least, I would have at least come with you to hold your hand."

That was exactly why she hadn't told him. He would take over like he always did and she would let him. She knew she relied too much on Trent. All of them did. Trent had basically raised all the Crosby children while Sheila was busy with her affairs and her position in society and Jack was busy building a business and carrying on plenty of affairs of his own.

She loved Trent deeply but after Ivy married a few months earlier, Katie realized perhaps she relied on him too much. She needed to stand on her own as Ivy had done, to find her own strength. The surgery was something she'd been thinking about for a long time and she wanted to do it alone. She didn't regret it for a second; she could see better now than she ever dreamed possible.

"I didn't want to bother you since I know how busy you've been with the super-router project."

He opened his mouth to argue—probably something about how he was never too busy for his little sister—but before he could utter a word, his name came over the loudspeaker.

"Will Mr. Trent Crosby approach the podium, please? Trent Crosby."

Katie turned and saw a woman she knew casually, Jenny Hall, giving the announcement.

Trent made a face. "Maybe I'll luck out and they're going to tell me they don't need to put me on the auction block after all."

She laughed. "You volunteered, buster. I think you're stuck."

He studied her for a moment. "You look good, Katie. If you can manage to fight off all the men who are going to be clamoring around you, save me a dance, okay?"

"Of course. Good luck."

She watched him go to the dais, then scanned the room looking for someone else she knew. The panic that had abated somewhat in Trent's presence bubbled back. This had to be the craziest idea she'd ever had, she thought again, nabbing her second—or was it third?—glass of champagne off a tray.

Whatever possessed her to think a little window dressing would cover her basic inadequacies? Her shyness, her social fumbling? She was one of those people who faded into the background and usually that was just the way she liked it.

It hadn't taken therapy for her to figure out it was a learned behavior, developed early when she discovered that if she could manage to avoid attention, Sheila's mercurial moods and sudden rages would rarely be aimed in her direction.

Trent wanted her here but she wished for once she could have said no to him. As much as she loved him, sometimes her older brother could be as forceful in his way as their father. She should have told him she couldn't come and stayed home in her little condo in Lake Oswego, where she was comfortable and boring and *safe*.

She should leave, she thought. Really, her obligation here was done. Trent needed moral support and she had given it. This whole idea was ridiculous. Childish. Even if she saw Steve Larson, he probably wouldn't care about any of this—the vision surgery, the blond highlights in her hair, the designer dress. He had the beautiful, though poisonous, Angelina on his arm.

She was about to set her glass on yet another tray carried by one of the ubiquitous waiters and make her escape when a tall man in an elegant black tuxedo approached her.

She recognized him instantly. Of course she knew who he was, since his younger self had starred in most of her adolescent fantasies—Peter Logan, oldest son of Terrence and Leslie Logan, and CEO of Crosby Systems's biggest competitor, Logan Corporation.

She waited for a spark of recognition, then the inevitable cold disdain once he realized she was one of the despised Crosbys. But all she could see in his eyes was frank male appreciation.

For her! Peter Logan was looking at shy, dowdy, plump Katie Crosby like he wanted to devour her from top to bottom.

No, not plump anymore, she reminded herself. After the debacle of her short-lived engagement, she had worked fiendishly hard to whip herself into shape. Instead of the comfort foods she had survived on since her lonely boarding school days, she began to eat a healthier diet and to exercise obsessively.

It took her three years of hard work but she hadn't been Steve Larson's cash cow for a long time, even if she still preferred dressing in baggy clothes and hiding behind thick glasses and long hair.

He smiled at her, then, before she realized what was happening, he gripped her arm and maneuvered her onto the dance floor. Despite her shock at his high-handedness, she couldn't help laughing. "Smooth. Very smooth. I see your reputation is not unfounded, Mr. Logan."

To her shock, her voice sounded sultry, smoky, like cognac trickling into a heavy crystal tumbler. Probably because she couldn't seem to breathe with him so close, with his expensive cologne filling her senses and his fingers entwined with hers.

"Ah, no fair. You know my name," he murmured, with what she almost thought looked like resignation in his eyes. She studied him for a moment, wondering at it. Perhaps the charmed life of a wealthy, successful bachelor wasn't as carefree as the world liked to believe.

"Peter Logan, CEO of Logan Corporation," she murmured, her mind on the memory of another long-ago dance and an act of great kindness he had done for a fat, miserable fifteen-year-old girl at her first society event.

"What woman in Portland hasn't seen a picture of you in the society pages," she went on, "and longed to be magically transformed into the latest elegant creature at your side?"

Where did this sudden flirtatiousness come from? she wondered, stunned at herself. She didn't think she even knew *how* to flirt! She also hadn't realized this fantasy of dancing again with him had been lurking inside her all these years.

"Since you know who I am, it's only fair you tell me your name, then. And address and marital status while you're at it. Oh, and are you free tomorrow night?"

She laughed and opened her mouth to answer, then snapped it closed again. Suddenly she didn't want to tell him who she was. When she did—when he knew the woman in his arms was none other than Katherine Crosby—that warm, appreciative light would disappear and he would turn cold and angry.

Like the rest of his family, Peter Logan had no love for the Crosbys. She knew well the bitter history behind Portland's most famous feud. Once the two families had been neighbors—and if not precisely friends, at least more than passing acquaintances. Her older brother Danny had been best friends with Peter's parents' son, Robbie.

One day when she'd been little more than an infant, Robbie had been playing at their house, theoretically under the watchful eye of Sheila.

But with her typical selfish carelessness, Sheila had paid little attention to the two boys. Sometime in the course of the day a stranger had approached them and Robbie had been kidnapped.

After an agonizing year of searching, a child's remains were found along a riverbank and were traced back to Robbie, allowing the Logans to at least have that much closure.

If Sheila had shown the tiniest ounce of remorse, Katie was sure that while Peter's parents might not have been able to forgive her mother for her inattention to the boys, Terrence and Leslie Logan likely would have kept their bitterness to themselves. But Katie's mother had tried to paint herself as the injured party, had blamed everyone for Robbie Logan's kidnapping except herself.

Over the years, the feud had taken on a life of its own. The Logans and the Crosbys were fierce competitors in business and cold as Alaskan tundra when they were forced to meet socially.

She had always grieved for the brother Peter never

knew. But then, he had been adopted after Robbie's kidnapping. Perhaps if the events of that horrible day had never happened, the Logans wouldn't have had any interest in adopting a child.

"This is the first time I've made a woman forget her own name."

At Peter's remark, she realized he was still waiting for an answer. "I didn't forget," she murmured.

"Just trying to decide whether to share it with me, then?"

She mustered a smile. "Something like that."

"I'm completely harmless, I promise. Ask anyone."

"I'm not sure your business rivals would agree."

His shrug barely rippled the silk of his well-cut tuxedo. "That's their problem, isn't it?"

She didn't want this to end. Not yet. A beautiful woman in a glittery blue dress was singing a sultry version of an old Duke Ellington song, and Katie wanted to burn this memory into her mind.

"Celeste," she finally said, seizing on her middle name. "My name is Celeste."

"Aw, the French. *C'est magnifique*." To her shock, he drew their clasped hands to his mouth and pressed his lips firmly to the first knuckle of her index finger. Heat sizzled through her and she couldn't believe she was actually here, in his arms.

Though Peter Logan had a reputation as a man who enjoyed the company of beautiful women, Katie never would have suspected him capable of this playful, sin-

gle-minded pursuit. She knew him as a hard busi-
nessman, ruthless and aggressive about increasing his
company's market share, no matter what it took.

She didn't know how to resist him like this. She
couldn't think straight when he looked at her out of
those deep brown eyes. Maybe if she had a clearer
head, she could summon some kind of defense, but
she had never had much tolerance for alcohol and she
suddenly feared she'd had one too many glasses of
champagne.

"I hope this isn't unforgivably rude but have we
met before? You seem familiar."

A knot formed in her stomach as she waited for him
to recognize her, but he only continued gazing at her
features intently. How could she answer that? She finally decided on the truth, or at least part of it. "Many
years ago we danced together at another one of these
society functions. I'm sure you wouldn't remember."

"I'm sorry. I should."

"Don't apologize. I've changed a great deal since
then." The understatement of the century, she
thought.

He twirled her around, his arms strong and commanding. He was a wonderful dancer, but she already knew that from the first time they had danced.
And though she would never be graceful, she had to
hope she had improved a little in thirteen years.

"Are you bidding tonight?" Peter asked. "If you
are, let me give you a little advice. Stay away from

my brother Eric. He's not worth what he'll end up costing you and will only end up breaking your heart."

She arched an eyebrow. "And I suppose you're going to tell me you would be the better bargain."

"I'm not up for bid this year. Eric is the only Logan on the auction block. I did my duty last year and ended up being purchased by Dorothea Aldridge. The woman in the purple turban over there."

Katie laughed. She didn't have to follow his gaze to know the woman in question. Dorothea's late husband left her a twelve-state restaurant chain. She had a passion for bridge, and she was old enough to be his great-grandmother. "What's the matter? Was she too much woman for you?"

He made a face. "I had to spend an entire Saturday playing cards and admiring photos of her grandchildren."

He paused, then added with a rueful smile. "You know, the really sad thing is, that Saturday with Dorothea was the most enjoyable date I've had in a long time."

She wasn't sure how to respond to that honest admission. She certainly couldn't tell him she hadn't been on a date in far longer than she wanted to think about.

"I'm not bidding," she finally said. "I'm only here as moral support to—" *My brother,* she started to say, but knew that would only raise questions she didn't want to answer. "A friend," she amended.

"A good friend?"

"Yes. Very good."

"Will this good friend—or anyone else, for that matter—mind that you're dancing with me?"

Trent would not be at all thrilled to see her dancing with Peter Logan. She was grateful they had moved to a darkened corner of the ballroom where they were out of the public eye. Maybe her brother would be too busy at the dais to notice them together. One could only hope.

"I can always tell him you kidnapped me before I knew what was happening," she murmured somewhat breathlessly when the last sultry notes of the jazz combo faded away.

"When a beautiful woman crosses my path, I'm not stupid enough to give her any chance to slip away."

Beautiful? Her? Awkward, pathetic Katie Crosby? Her heart did a little joyful dance in her chest and Katie decided if a typhoon swept through the Portland Hilton at exactly that moment, she would at least die a happy woman.

"I'm afraid that's just what I'm going to do. Slip away, I mean. I have to go find my…friend."

She had to admit, some small corner of her heart found his disappointed expression extremely gratifying. Maybe this idea to glam up for once wasn't so dumb after all, not if she could have this memory of dancing with him again after she faded once more into the background.

"I'd like to see you again somewhere a little less formal." He grabbed her hand before she could leave. "How can I reach you?"

She studied him as the crowd began gathering near the dais, trying to figure out how to answer that. She couldn't lie and tell him she wasn't interested in seeing him again. This was Peter Logan. No woman with a pulse would be able to honestly say she didn't want to see him again!

When she was younger, all the girls she knew had swooned over him, with his dark, slightly dangerous good looks and that intensity in his brown eyes. She had treasured the memory of that long-ago dance as one of the highlights of her adolescence.

What girl wouldn't have been thrilled to have him ride to her rescue like some gorgeous knight in shining armor, vanquishing all the dragons in his path—or in her case, Angelina Mitchell, now Larson, and some of her friends, who had cornered Katie during a benefit like this one and were mocking her relentlessly.

No, she couldn't tell him she didn't want to see him but she had to think of some evasion. Before she could, someone jostled her hard from behind. She would have fallen if Peter's arms hadn't come around her.

"Excuse me, dear," she heard a quavering voice say. "I'm terribly sorry. Are you all right?"

Katie turned to see who had bumped into her and found Dorothea Aldridge, purple turban and all.

"Dorothea?" Peter said. "Are you all right? You're looking a little pale."

She squinted at him. "Is that you, Peter Logan?"

"Yes. Is everything all right?"

"I'm just a little warm, dear. I was looking for a place to sit down and lost my balance. Too many people pushing and shoving for someone with a bad hip."

Katie realized everyone was heading toward the podium and she assumed the bachelor auction was about to begin.

"Let's find you a chair," Peter said. He offered his arm to Mrs. Aldridge and without prompting, Katie moved to the elderly woman's other side.

"Have we met, dear?" Dorothea asked as they made their way through the crowd to a row of chairs along the edge of the ballroom.

Only about a hundred times at various functions. Katie's stomach plummeted and she knew the game was up. She would have to identify herself and watch that exhilarating attraction in Peter's eyes fade to something else entirely.

"I—" She started to speak but Peter cut her off.

"This is Celeste," he said as he settled Mrs. Aldridge into a chair with a gentleness that did funny things to Katie's insides.

"How lovely to meet you," Dorothea said with a bleary-eyed smile. "And may I say, that's a lovely mink hat you're wearing. I have one just like it myself. My dear husband, Victor, gave it to me a few years before he passed. A little stuffy in here for fur, though, don't you think?"

Katie raised her eyebrows and fought the urge to run a hand over the head she knew perfectly well was bare.

"Where are your glasses, Dorothea?" Peter asked, laughter in his voice.

"Oh, I'm a silly old thing and left them up in my room."

"You're staying here?" he asked.

"Oh, yes. I do every year for the Children's Connection auction. I make a whole weekend out of it. It's the highlight of my year. Drat. I can't see who I'm bidding on. Since I heard you're not available this year, I had my eye on that brother of yours. Eric. He's quite the hottie, as my granddaughters would say. Peter, would you be a love and fetch my glasses for me? I think I left them on the bedside table."

"Of course."

"Oh, thank you! You're such a sweet boy. You always have been."

She said this with such sincerity that Katie had to bite her lip to keep from laughing. Peter Logan, sweet? She didn't hear that term bandied about much when it came to Peter. The man was a shark in the boardroom and everybody knew it.

He might have occasional bouts of kindness but otherwise he was hard and driven, completely focused on expanding the Logan empire.

"Now here's my room key," Mrs. Aldridge said. "I'm in suite 1460 and my glasses should be on the bedside table. Hurry now, before Eric and all the other good-looking fellows are gone."

"My feet are wings," Peter assured her with the smile that had fluttered the heart of more than one society matron, then headed out of the ballroom, tugging Katie along with him.

He was holding so tightly to her arm, she had no choice but to follow him. "I don't believe it takes both of us to fetch one pair of glasses," she exclaimed.

"I decided I'm not letting you go."

Ever? she wondered as a thrill shot through her. This was all pretend, she reminded herself. If he knew who she was, he would drop her arm so fast her head would spin.

"You're very used to getting your own way, aren't you?" she asked in the elevator.

His laugh was heartfelt and slid down her spine. "Do you have brothers or sisters, Celeste?"

"I…yes. Both."

"Then you'll understand when I say that with two brothers and two sisters, I learned early to hang on tightly to anything I didn't particularly want to share."

"Should I be flattered that I'm apparently in the same category as a favorite toy, Mr. Logan?"

"No, you're not." He grinned. "You're much better than G.I. Joe and Stretch Armstrong combined."

She laughed. "I'm sure you wouldn't have thought so when you were ten."

"I don't know. I was a pretty smart kid."

He was, she knew. He had earned top grades at prep school and went on to graduate from Harvard with honors.

The elevator slid smoothly to a stop on the fourteenth floor before she could respond, and Peter led the way to room 1460.

The glasses weren't where Dorothea had claimed. All they found on the bedside table was a box of tissues and a pill keeper marked with the days of the week.

"Any ideas where to look?" Peter asked.

"The bathroom, maybe?"

He left her in the bedroom of the suite but returned a moment later. "No luck. We'd better hurry and find them or Dorothea might end up missing out on the bidding altogether."

"We certainly wouldn't want that."

Though she felt a little uncomfortable poking through someone else's hotel suite, she remembered what a dear Mrs. Aldridge was. If she enjoyed being in the company of younger men—and gave generously to the Children's Connection in the process—Katie didn't want to disappoint her.

After a few moments of fruitless searching, she glanced through the sliding doors toward the glittering city lights just beyond the small covered terrace.

It had been a lovely day, unusually mild for December. Perhaps Dorothea had decided to enjoy it while she awaited the big night. She slid open the doors and immediately saw a folded newspaper on the small table—along with a pair of glasses on a jeweled chain.

"I've got them," she called out, then was surprised when he answered her from the doorway.

"Good sleuthing. I never would have thought to look out here. Who's crazy enough to spend any time on the balcony of a hotel during a Portland December?"

"We're here, aren't we?" she said with a smile.

"That's different. We're doing a favor for a friend."

"And enjoying the view," she pointed out, gesturing to the glittering city lights below them. "I love looking at the city lights, especially with everything decorated for the holidays. It's gorgeous up here."

"Yes, it is," he said, his voice low, and Katie felt heat flood her face when she realized he wasn't looking at the view but at her.

"Um, we should be getting back, I suppose. Dorothea, er, Mrs. Aldridge, will be looking for these."

"I warned you I was an opportunist. When I find myself alone on a starlit balcony with a beautiful woman, I'd be a fool not to take advantage of it."

Before she realized what he intended, he leaned closer, then lowered his mouth to hers.

Peter Logan was kissing her! She could hardly be-

lieve it. It was an easy kiss, almost casual, the kind
a man would give to a good friend. Later she thought
maybe he only intended a quick buss but the moment
their mouths collided, heat burned between them,
like brilliant sunlight glimmering on the ocean, and
they both lost control.

She wasn't aware of sliding her arms around his
neck but she must have because somehow her fingers
were in his thick hair, her achy breasts pressed tightly
against him.

He groaned and deepened the kiss and she was
vaguely aware of his hands, hot and firm, sliding down
the bare skin of her back to press her closer to him. She
could feel his arousal through the silk of his trousers
and couldn't believe it. Peter Logan wanted her!

"You taste incredible," he murmured against her
mouth. "I'll never drink champagne again without
thinking of this moment."

She was afraid she wouldn't be able to ever *breathe*
again without remembering this magical night. It
would be forever burned into her consciousness.

She tightened her hold around his neck and kissed
him fiercely with all the passion inside her.

She would have stayed there all night—Mrs. Aldridge's glasses be damned—but suddenly something
odd registered in her dazed awareness, a bright flash
of light.

She drew back slightly. "Did you see that?"

"What?" His voice sounded dazed and when he

opened his eyes, they were dark and aroused and didn't stray from her face.

"Was that lightning?"

"It couldn't be. The sky is clear."

Katie realized now that must have been the moment the *Portland Weekly* photographer caught them kissing. He must have followed them from the ballroom and slipped out onto the public terrace next to them. At the time, she thought it must have been just a product of her overactive imagination— or the result of too little oxygen to her brain from Peter's kiss.

Whatever it was, the distraction reminded her of where they were, what she was doing—kissing a man who would hate her if he ever learned her name. "I…Mrs. Aldridge will be looking for her eyeglasses."

"Why don't we forget about the glasses and stay here for the rest of the night?"

"We can't do that. You promised you'd take them right back."

With a heavy sigh, he dropped his arms and stepped away from her. For the first time since coming out on the balcony, Katie felt chilled in the cold December air. She rubbed her bare arms.

"I'm a selfish bastard to keep you out here so long in that thin dress. Come on, let's go find Dorothea."

He held her hand on the elevator but they were

joined by another couple and he didn't try to kiss her again.

She didn't want to go back inside the ballroom, Katie realized on the way back to the main floor.

For one thing, when Peter gave Mrs. Aldridge back her glasses, Katie knew the woman would recognize her immediately, makeover or not, and then Peter would know he had just spent several very heated moments with a Crosby in his arms.

For another, she wanted to remember this night just as it was. She didn't want to go inside the ballroom and have to make polite conversation when all she wanted to do was go home and hug her arms around herself and remember what it had been like to have Peter Logan want her!

Outside the ballroom, she scrambled to come up with an excuse for not accompanying him to Dorothea's side. "I need to find the ladies' room and repair my lipstick."

He looked reluctant to have her leave his side. "Will you meet me right back here, then, after I deliver these to Dorothea?"

She couldn't think of an excuse not to meet him so she simply nodded, fighting the urge to cross her fingers at the lie.

As soon as he went inside the ballroom, she hurried to the hotel's porte cochere, feeling again like Cinderella escaping the ball.

Unfortunately her pumpkin wasn't waiting for

her. She couldn't see the Crosby driver Trent had sent for her in the row of limousines lined up outside and was forced to wait while the doorman paged him.

She wasn't able to escape so easily. Five moments later, her ride still hadn't appeared and her heart sank when she spied Peter hurrying through the lobby.

"You're leaving?" he asked when he reached her, disbelief and something else that sounded suspiciously like hurt in his voice.

She cleared her throat. "I was, ah, feeling a little under the weather. I think I had a little too much champagne." That was at least true enough.

To her relief, he didn't question her claim. "Are you waiting for a taxi? My driver is right there. I'll drop you off."

"You can't want to leave the gala so early."

"Can't I?"

That sizzling heat was back in his eyes and she couldn't help feeling tremendously flattered. He would rather drive her home than stay at a benefit for his family's pet charity.

"I can't let you take me home. You have obligations here."

"No, I don't. I told you this year was my brother's turn. The only obligation I made was to show up and I did that. Now I'm free to leave."

She opened her mouth to argue with him just as she spied her driver pulling into the entrance in one of the Crosby Systems's limousines, complete with the discreet company logo on the side. When Peter saw her climb inside, he would figure out immediately who she was.

"Okay," she said quickly and headed toward the Logan limousine he'd gestured to earlier. "Let's go, then."

He followed her, looking a little disconcerted at her rapid about-face. He opened the door for her and she slid inside.

And sealed her fate.

Four

What time was it? Katie had no idea since she had unplugged her alarm clock to conserve power and her watch was somewhere jammed into her suitcase, but she assumed it was long after midnight.

The storm still raged outside, hurling snow at the windows and moaning under the eaves. The room was cool and she realized while she'd been lost in the past, she had let the fire burn down to embers.

She rose from the bed and threw another log on the glowing cinders, then stood in front of the fireplace watching the flames leap to consume new fuel with fierce, enthusiastic crackles.

Her hand went to her abdomen, to the tiny life she

had only learned was growing there a few days before but already loved so dearly.

Oh, Katie, she thought with a sigh. *What a mess you've created, all because you got carried away by the magic of the night and caught up in your own lies.*

In the limousine that night, Peter had asked where he could drop her. For the first time, she realized the trouble her spontaneity had gotten her into. What was she supposed to tell him? She couldn't very well give him her address in Lake Oswego. Though he likely had no idea where Katherine Crosby lived, her last name was on the mailbox of her town house.

"Can't we just drive for a while?"

"I thought you were feeling under the weather."

Caught in another lie. She grimaced and improvised quickly. "It must have been the crowds at the benefit. I'm fine now."

"Good," he said. His smile was just short of wolfish but it still sent sensual little shivers rippling down her spine.

He leaned forward to talk to the chauffeur. "Lou, it's a lovely night for a drive."

The driver, a man in his late fifties with a bushy salt-and-pepper mustache, smiled back at him. "It is indeed, Mr. Logan."

"The lady likes Christmas lights. Maybe you could show us some of the holiday decorations around town if you know of any particularly festive spots."

"I surely do," the driver said with a cheerful wink in the rearview mirror at Katie.

She lost track of time there in that limousine. They drove all over Portland talking and laughing and drinking champagne as the limousine driver took them to one brightly decorated spot after another.

With each sip of champagne, she felt her natural restraints melt away. When Peter raised the privacy barrier behind the chauffeur and kissed her again, all the heat from before on the balcony flared to life again. She had never known anything like that, had been outside of her head with desire, and she never wanted to stop.

She must have murmured something to that effect because in between more of those mind-numbing kisses he asked if she would go home with him. To her surprise, she heard herself eagerly agree.

They barely made it inside his vast loft before they were ripping clothes away and coming together in a fiery explosion. They had made love in every corner of his loft, she remembered now, flushing a little when she remembered her uninhibited response to him. Her breasts, now sensitive and achy from hormones, tingled at the memories flooding through her mind.

They had used protection every time but one, she remembered. She had slept a little and had awakened to find he had turned to her in his sleep. He awakened, poised to enter her. That time had been tender and slow and incredibly sensuous. And condomless, she remembered, although he had pulled out before his orgasm.

After he finally fell fully asleep, the enormity of what she had done hit her like a building crumbling around her head. She had slept with Peter Logan, not once but four times! It had been the most wonderful, magical night of her life.

And he didn't even know her name.

She had spent the last three months trying to forget, but the memory of that night was scored into her mind like circuits on a motherboard.

For a woman who had graduated summa cum laude from Stanford, it was remarkable how stupid she could be, she thought now as she gazed into the flames.

When she missed her first period, she hadn't really been surprised. She'd always had irregular periods, especially during times of stress. And even when it was regular, she had a longer than usual cycle. After she missed the second period, she started to become concerned but still it never even occurred to her that she might be pregnant until her breasts started to ache at even the slightest pressure and she started throwing up in the mornings.

This should be such a happy time. It was, she assured herself. She was excited about the challenge and joy of motherhood. But part of her yearned to have someone to share her excitement with.

She couldn't tell Peter, she thought again. If her resolve started to waver, she only had to look around her at this house her father had bought for one of his mistresses. Not because he thought his children would enjoy a ranch or because he wanted to spend time with them here, but for a woman. It was so typical of Jack.

Everything she knew about Peter told her he was cut from the same cloth. Maybe not the womanizing part, but his obsession would always be Logan Corporation. Something else would always come before his child, just as work and women had come first for her father.

She couldn't do that to her child. She *wouldn't*.

With a sigh, she returned to bed and pulled the quilt around her chin once more. She lay there for a long time, listening to the wind moan and trying not to want what she knew she could never have.

Peter awoke quickly, as he always did, his mind already racing with a dozen things requiring his attention. The board of directors meeting in a week, the paperwork for a new merger Logan was considering, the marketing plan for the super-router.

He was unlikely to accomplish any of those things while he was stuck here at some godforsaken Wyoming ranch house with the deceitful, manipulative Katherine Crosby, however.

He sighed and watched his breath puff out in a lit-

tle cloud. In a *freezing* godforsaken ranch house, he
amended. A gust of wind rattled the wide picture window that probably had a spectacular view under normal conditions. All he could see now in the pale early-
morning light was snow. It was a virtual whiteout.

A glance at the huge river-rock fireplace in the
gathering room showed him the fire was all but out.
The temperature had dipped even colder in the night.
Why hadn't the furnace clicked on, he wondered?
Maybe the oil lines were frozen somehow or the pilot
light had gone out. He would have to take a look at
it this morning. What was the point of having a generator if they couldn't keep the furnace running?

For now he could at least work on the fire. He rose
and selected a log from the supply next to the fireplace
and tossed it onto the embers. He had to spend a few
moments stoking it to get any sparks but after a moment the wood caught and began to burn merrily.

He didn't have time for this, he thought as he
watched the flames. He had enough figurative fires
of his own to tend to. Logan was at a critical point
with this super-router, poised to make huge market
gains. Besides that project, he had at least a dozen
other items awaiting his attention.

He could only imagine what his family would say
when he turned up missing. He had mentioned his
destination to a few people, including his secretary,
and had filed a flight plan, but he hadn't told his parents or any of his siblings. He didn't know if they

would believe he could drop everything to chase after Katie Crosby.

Hell, he could hardly believe it himself. He had a reputation as someone who always kept a cool head, no matter the crisis. He had worked hard for that, had prided himself on his self-possession in tough circumstances. It was a skill he had picked up from his father, one necessary to run a huge company like Logan Corporation.

He wasn't exactly sure how he'd completely lost that cool head he was supposed to have. His brother Eric might take off after a woman on a whim like this but not Peter. Peter had spent his whole life trying to show he was responsible, dependable. He just wasn't the sort to let his emotions dictate his actions.

But he hadn't been himself since the moment his gaze met Katie's at the Children's Connection auction. It sounded corny when he tried to put it into words but that whole night seemed surreal, like something out of an incredibly erotic dream. Instant heat, complete enchantment.

What about her had affected him so strongly that night? She had been elegantly beautiful, but he had certainly dated his share of beautiful women. No, there was something more, something he still couldn't quite put his finger on.

Maybe it was that she hadn't seemed particularly impressed that he was one of the wealthiest, most powerful men in Portland. Or maybe it had been the

way she seemed completely oblivious to her own
appeal, or that soft, genuine smile of hers that had
seemed fresh and almost innocent.

Whatever had mesmerized him, he still couldn't
believe the spontaneous attraction between them. He
enjoyed the company of women but that night had
been different.

It had been a night of firsts for him—the first time
he'd ever blown off a charity obligation, the first
time he had ever driven around Portland with a
woman just to look at Christmas lights, the first time
he had ever taken a woman he had just met back to
his apartment for an all-night session of lovemaking.

He hadn't intended to. It wasn't at all like him.
When he'd offered her a ride home, all he'd been
thinking about was flirting with her a little, finding
out where she lived so he could make plans to see her
again. Maybe stealing a kiss or two. But she had
kissed him with such eager, wild abandon, he hadn't
been able to think about anything but touching her,
tasting her, coming inside her.

He blew out a breath. He had wanted Celeste—
Katherine Crosby—with a fierceness he had never
known before. Their lovemaking had been the most
intense of his life, fiery and hot one moment, slow
and sensual the next. Nothing in his experience had
prepared him for that kind of stomach-clenching heat.

And then she disappeared.

He could still vividly recall the hard knot of betrayal that had lodged in his gut when he had awakened to find her gone. If it hadn't been for her soft perfume clinging to tangled sheets, and a polite note that could have been written by a stranger, he would have thought maybe it had all been some wild dream, the kind of thing he thought he'd outgrown when he left adolescence behind.

He had searched the loft for something she might have left behind, something that might help him trace her, but had found nothing. All that day he had paced his apartment, overwhelmed with the feeling that he had held something rare and precious in his hands for one fleeting second and then let it slip away.

That odd feeling of loss was the real reason he was so angry at her now, he acknowledged. He had been such a gullible fool. He had believed she had been as caught up in the magic of the night as he was, had wanted him just as fiercely as he had her, when she had only been using him as a pawn in this bitter feud between their families.

He hated thinking of the way he had missed her these three months. How could he miss a woman he had just met, one he didn't really even know? He hated remembering how for three long months, with no solid clue how to find her, he waited for her to contact him, looking for her as discreetly as possible.

That damn picture in the *Weekly* hadn't helped matters. How could he ask questions about the woman—like, oh, maybe her *name*—after the picture of them in a passionate embrace was plastered all over the paper?

In a million years, he never would have connected his Celeste to Katherine Crosby.

Since the moment he had seen the article identifying her the day before, he had been racking his brain trying to remember if they had ever met before the night of the gala. He had to think they must have bumped into each other at some function or other. Portland wasn't that big and, despite the infamous enmity between the families, the Crosbys and Logans moved in the same circles. How had he completely overlooked her?

He thought he remembered her as someone who tended to lurk in the background. He knew she was the vice president of research and development at Crosby Systems, but other than that, he thought maybe she was almost as reclusive as her brother, Danny, who was holed up on some island in Hawaii.

If someone had asked him a week ago about Katherine Crosby, he would have been hard-pressed to come up with a description, but he thought maybe she used to wear thick glasses and had long, bushy hair that all but hid her face. Had she been a little plump? Damn it, he couldn't remember. All he could picture was the lithe, sensual woman who had completely ensnared him the night of the gala.

And now here they were holed up together at some Wyoming ranch. Katherine Crosby, with her baggy sweater and her wool socks, hardly seemed like the elegant creature he had flirted with and danced with and kissed on a moonlit balcony. This woman was quiet, almost nervous around him.

She *should* be nervous, he thought. He couldn't remember ever being so furious at another human being before.

What was he going to do about it? He had no real evidence she had stolen anything from him that night. He couldn't press charges, even if he wanted to. He didn't. Bringing it all out into the open would only expose what a gullible idiot he'd been.

So what could he do? Nothing. Not one damn thing. The knowledge didn't sit well with him at all, not for a man used to seizing control of every situation.

He would have to wait out this storm for the next day or so, just until he could return to Portland and try to figure out just how much damage his stupid indiscretion had cost the company—and the family—he loved so dearly.

It irked him to lift a finger here to help a Crosby, but he wasn't any good at inactivity so he decided to take a look at the furnace while he waited for her to awaken.

He changed out of the sweats he'd slept in and into jeans and a sweater then headed for the utility room off the back porch where they had started the generator earlier.

The generator still hummed away. He checked the fuel level and saw the tank was still nearly full, so he turned his attention to the furnace. As he suspected, the pilot light had somehow gone out in the night, he soon discovered. It only took him a moment to re-light it, and he was rewarded with the click and whir of the furnace coming to life.

That chore out of the way, he returned to the kitchen to put on some coffee. He was just pouring a cup when Katherine came in from her bedroom. She had changed into another pair of jeans, slightly less disreputable than the pair she'd been wearing the day before, and a Stanford sweatshirt.

"Good morning," she murmured, just enough sleepy huskiness in her voice to make him wonder what it would have been like to wake up with that sexy voice next to him.

"Have you looked outside yet?" he asked gruffly, angry at his instant response to her. "I don't think *good morning* really applies here."

She glanced out the kitchen window and grimaced. "It's freezing in here."

"Your pilot light on the furnace went out. I just lit it again. It should warm up in a minute."

Surprise flickered in her brown eyes. "Um, thank you. You've been busy this morning."

"Coffee's fresh if you'd like some."

She shook her head. "I'd better not. Thanks, though. I'll have some herbal tea."

She was riffling through the cupboards looking for it—and he was trying to figure out why she wouldn't have coffee when there had been clear longing in her voice—when he heard the low rumble of an approaching motor. A snowmobile, by the sound of it.

"That would be Darwin Simmons from the Bar S. He's taking care of the stock while Clint and Margie are gone."

A moment later the front doorbell rang. Katherine went to answer it and Peter followed her. She answered the door and he saw a heavily bundled figure in a thick snowmobile suit, only two blue eyes showing out of all the winter gear.

Katherine gestured the figure inside and Peter had the feeling he was much younger than he expected. That impression was confirmed when the figure removed his heavy wool face mask, revealing a teenager of no more than fourteen or fifteen.

Peter had an impression of wiry strength and the kind of competence that seemed bred into the bones of children raised on ranches.

"Joseph!" Katherine Crosby exclaimed. "I wasn't expecting you. Is your father outside?"

"No, ma'am. He's home. We lost part of the roof on one of the hay sheds last night. Dad was working on it and slipped off."

"Oh, no!"

Peter wondered at the genuine distress he thought he saw on her features. He hardly would have expected her to be concerned for a neighbor to her family's hobby ranch, one she probably barely knew.

"Is he all right?" Katherine asked.

"No, ma'am," the boy said again. "Doc Harp met us at the clinic to X-ray it and she said his leg is broke in two places. He's got to stay off it for the next couple months. Dad was real worried about you over here, what with the Taylors gone and the storm and all, so he sent me to help out. Hope that's okay with you."

"No! No, it's not okay."

Peter narrowed his gaze. There was the spoiled rich bitch he would have expected. She didn't have to throw a tantrum about not getting her own way. Not when the kid was only trying to help. He was about to intervene when she went on quickly, surprising him again.

"With your father hurt, I'm sure you must be needed at home, aren't you? The Bar S is much bigger than Sweetwater."

"My dad said I'm to help you out. Feed and water the stock and so forth."

"You tell your father not to spend a minute worrying about me over here," she said. "You need to be with your family. I can take care of things here."

He paused, fingering his wool cap, worry on his young features. "A hay bale can be mighty heavy. No offense, Ms. Crosby, but are you sure a little thing like you can handle things here by yourself?"

"I'm hardly a little thing, Joseph," she said with a laugh. "Anyway, I won't be by myself. This is my, um, my…"

Her voice trailed off and for some ridiculous reason, Peter found it amusing that she couldn't quite come up with a word to classify him.

"My friend, Peter Logan," she finally said. "He can help me."

He was further amused to find himself on the receiving end of a skeptical look from the kid, who undoubtedly figured he was some worthless city yuppie.

"You know anything about cattle, sir?" the boy asked.

He knew he liked his steaks medium-rare, but that was about it. He wasn't about to confess, though. "Enough," he lied. He gave a confident, take-charge kind of smile to set the kid's mind at rest. "We'll be just fine. Ms. Crosby's right. A man's got to look after his family first."

The boy still looked unconvinced, but Katie ushered him out the door so smoothly Peter didn't think he was even aware of it. "You go on home and help your mother and brother with your own livestock," she said. "If we run into trouble, we'll call you. I promise."

He was clearly torn between obeying his father and taking care of the many chores at the Bar S. Finally he nodded, though he still looked worried. "My dad said Mr. Taylor should have left a note in the tack room with instructions on how much to feed the horses and how much hay to take out to the cattle.

You'll have to also make sure the trough heaters are working so the drinking water doesn't freeze."

Since the ranch caretaker was so organized that he left detailed notes about starting a generator, Peter wasn't at all surprised to learn he had left the same kind of clear instructions for watering and feeding the stock.

"We'll be fine," Katherine assured him again. "You tell your father not to worry a minute about us. Tell him to save his energy for healing that leg of his."

"I'll do that, ma'am."

With one last worried look, the boy disappeared once more inside his winter gear, mounted the snow-mobile at the bottom of the porch then roared off down the driveway.

"What now?" Peter asked when the throb of the sled's motor had faded to a distant roar.

She smiled, the first one she'd given him since his arrival the day before. "First we'd better find you something warmer than that leather jacket you came in. Then I guess we get to work."

She could do this.

Katie pulled on the warmest, thickest gloves she could find in the mudroom while she repeated the mantra to herself. She was a bright, healthy woman. She was strong, she was invincible, yada yada yada.

If she could keep from throwing up the half bagel she'd managed to choke down for breakfast, she just might make it through.

And if she could keep her mind away from the dangerous memory of how sleep-rumpled and sexy Peter Logan had looked that morning, she just might be able to control her chaotic hormones enough to keep her out of trouble.

You're already in a world of trouble, Katherine Celeste, a sly little voice in her head mocked.

But she didn't have to make things worse by doing something utterly stupid like falling in love with him. She could only be relieved that Peter despised her so she wasn't tempted to complicate the mess by sleeping with him again.

She *was* relieved, she told herself. It was better this way. Once the storm cleared, he would return to Portland and leave her alone. He would likely want nothing more to do with her. And she could think of no reason for their paths to cross again.

She would be free to have her child alone and he would never know their single night of passion had left any legacy behind.

She drew in a shaky breath, fighting off the sudden depression that had settled on her shoulders, colder and heavier than even eighteen inches of snow. She had no choice, she reminded herself, and walked into the great room to face him.

Despite her lingering nausea and the ache in her heart, she had to laugh at the picture he made. The Portland gossip columnists would have a tough time believing the man zipping into brown insulated coveralls was the same sexy, urbane CEO they loved to write about, the one who consistently made it on to Portland's Top Ten Best-Dressed list.

Peter was a big man but Clint was huge, both tall and broad. His coveralls on Peter bagged in every direction.

He looked up at the sound of her laughter. "At least they're roomy," he said with a wry look.

Maybe it was a stress release from the tension still simmering between them, but her laughter seemed to bubble out like water from a geyser. "Look at it this way," she said. "If there are any half-frozen calves out there, we'll know just where to put them to warm them up."

"You can just forget that idea right now. I'm not sharing. Any half-frozen calves will just have to find their own heat source."

He finished zipping up the coveralls, watching her with an odd light in his eyes as her laughter faded. "Okay, I'm ready," he said. "Are you sure you're up to this? You're still looking a little peaked. I can probably take care of things on my own."

So much for that vaunted pregnancy glow, Katie thought. She looked horrid and she knew it perfectly well. She just had to keep him from figuring out why.

"I'm fine. Let's go," she muttered, and led the way out into the teeth of the storm.

Five

Once they were outside, she wasn't surprised when Peter took over the lead, bearing the full brunt of the wind that cut like jagged glass, even through all the layers. Despite her six-foot-tall moving windbreak, the storm still hurled swirling snowflakes at her like tiny, sharp stones that stung her eyes and lodged in every exposed nook.

Peter shortened his stride through the knee-high snowdrifts to match hers so she was better able to walk in his footsteps. She was grateful for his thoughtfulness. It was hard enough fighting the wind without having to blaze a path through the snow.

The three hundred feet from the house to the

sturdy barn seemed to take an eternity to cross but at last they reached the door. Both of them worked another several moments clearing snow with their gloved hands away from the doorway so they could slide open the door.

By the time they made it inside, Katie was exhausted and queasy enough to fear the bagel would make a reappearance.

Peter pulled off his hat and gloves as Clint's two border collies greeted them with quick, well-mannered barks. He leaned down to pet one, shaking his head. "That storm is incredible. I've never seen anything like it!"

"Neither have I. I've been here a few times during storms but they were nothing like this. This is intense, even for western Wyoming. I can't believe it's March."

"Remind me to heed the weather forecast the next time I'm tempted to take off from Portland on a whim."

She wouldn't be around to remind him of anything, she thought with another pang. Back in the city, they would go their separate ways. He would return to the helm of Logan, probably still believing she stole company secrets. This interlude of theirs would probably add more fuel to the Logan-Crosby feud.

She hoped her baby never found out how much her father despised her mother.

"I suppose it's a good thing I did," Peter went on, scratching the other dog. "Come out here, I mean. You never could have handled this on your own."

She wasn't completely helpless. Really, she probably knew more about horses and cattle than he did from all the time she had spent out here. This further evidence of his poor opinion of her stung, she had to admit.

"I would have figured something out," she muttered.

He raised a skeptical eyebrow. "You would have been in one hell of a bind on your own out here and we both know it."

She would have had a rough time of it alone, she had to admit, especially with the nausea so close to the surface and the fatigue weighing her down. To say she was glad he'd come to Sweetwater would have been a gross exaggeration, so she opted to change the subject.

"Let's find out what we have to do, shall we? Joseph said Clint left the instructions in the tack room, right over here."

Clint kept the barn in ruthless order. Just like the rest of his domain, it was clean and well organized—no clutter, no loose hay, no scattered tools. The tack room was used as the ranch office. A huge, scarred pine desk with a computer dominated the room, along with a couple of worn armchairs and one entire wall hung with saddles and bridles and leads. The smell of leather and horses was heavy in the room.

They found the note addressed to Darwin Simmons on a bulletin board behind the desk, sandwiched between an invoice from the feed and grain in Jackson and a list of phone numbers.

Katie tugged off her gloves to pull the note down. Peter stood behind her to peer over her shoulder, and she was suddenly intensely conscious of his nearness. Heat emanated from him in the cool room. He had taken time for a quick shower before bundling into the winter gear and she could smell clean soap and some indefinable scent uniquely Peter.

Pregnancy had definitely made her sense of smell more acute. The scent of him, familiar and erotic, instantly transported her to the night they spent together, reminding her of tasting every inch of his skin, of inhaling that scent as he kissed her, of lying in his arms and feeling safe and warm and *wanted*.

Oh, how she craved that again.

The intense hunger came out of nowhere and she drew in a sharp breath. What was the matter with her? Peter despised her and thought she had tricked him like some corporate Mata Hari into sleeping with her only so she could worm out Logan secrets.

She was foolish to even think about their night together. It would never happen again and wanting the impossible only wasted energy she couldn't afford to expend. Might as well wish for that storm out there to suddenly stop, she thought. She had as much chance of controlling her thoughts as she did of controlling the weather.

Where was she? She had lost her place, she realized with chagrin. Even worse, her body had instinctively leaned back toward his, drawn by his heat and the invisible ties that bound them inexorably together. She jerked upright just before she would have settled against him, just as if she had every right to snuggle there.

Had he noticed? she wondered. How could he have missed the motion? Embarrassed color flooded her face and her gaze flew to his. She found him watching her, a disconcerted expression in his eyes.

He cleared his throat and stepped away, putting space between them. "It all looks fairly self-explanatory," he said. "I'll take care of the cattle, you can feed and water the horses."

She didn't register his words for a few moments, still lost in her mortification. When she did, her spine straightened and she forgot all about being embarrassed.

"Forget it," she said sharply. "You take care of the horses and I'll see to the cattle."

Sweetwater's dozen horses could all be fed and watered from inside the barn, but the small herd of cattle were pastured out in the open, in the middle of the wind and swirling snow.

"I'm taking care of the cattle," he said, his voice leaving no room for arguments.

She didn't let his hard tone stop her. "It's my family's ranch. I won't ask you to go out into that storm again, just to help a Crosby."

A muscle worked in his jaw, as if he didn't like

being reminded of her last name. "You didn't ask. I offered. No, I'm not offering, I'm insisting. Whether they're Crosby cattle or not, they still need to be fed."

"I can do it."

"You're a hell of a liar, *Celeste,* but even you won't be able to convince me you're able to haul a hundred-pound hay bale, not when I can tell you're still feeling under the weather."

She didn't like being reminded of how horrible she knew she must look—or the reason for it. "I would be doing everything myself if you hadn't come charging out to Sweetwater like some damn avenging angel. I can handle it. I'm tougher than I look."

"So am I. And if you want to see how tough I can really be, keep arguing."

She bristled. "Are you threatening me, Logan?"

He narrowed his gaze. "Damn right. Shut up or I'll lock you in this tack room until I'm done feeding all the cattle *and* the horses."

One look at his hard expression warned her he would make good on the threat. She blew out a frustrated breath but wasn't quite ready to give up. "You might run Logan with that iron fist of yours, but this ranch belongs to me and my family."

"I don't see anybody else here but you and me."

"Peter—"

"Give it up. You won't win this one." He headed for the door. "I'll meet you back here when I'm done."

"Take the dogs," she called out just before he went

outside. "They'll help you find your way back to the barn with this poor visibility."

After he left with Luke and Millie in the lead, she fought a completely childish urge to throw something at the door behind him or at least to stomp her boot on the plank floor.

He was right. That was the hardest pill to swallow. She wanted to think she was capable and self-sufficient, but deep in her heart, she knew she would have been in a terrible bind without him here. She *couldn't* carry a hay bale by herself, even a few hundred feet to the fenceline of the vast pasture where the cattle grazed.

She knew she would have figured something out—maybe she could have rigged up one of the horses to help haul the hay bales out—but it would have taken her hours to do everything. In her current condition, she would have been completely exhausted.

Still, he didn't need to be so high-handed. Threatening to lock her in the tack room of her own ranch!

After a few more moments of fuming—and willing her morning sickness to subside—she sighed and rose from Clint's chair. If she didn't get off the south side of her pants, as Clint would say, Peter would finish his share of the workload before she did hers, even though he had the bigger job. And wouldn't she just hate that?

For the next hour, she cleaned out stalls and forked fresh straw and checked the water in each trough. She put out feed according to Clint's instructions and made sure the dogs had food and water in their snug little corner of the barn.

In the process, her nausea receded, to her vast relief. She even started to enjoy being among the horses. She saved her favorite for last, a bay with the prosaic name of Susan.

Katie loved the little mare and rode her whenever she stayed at the ranch. Susan wasn't the flashiest of horses on the ranch or the quickest or the strongest, but she was sturdy and dependable.

When she neared the horse's stall, Susan whinnied a greeting and edged close for her expected treat.

"I didn't bring you anything this time, sweetheart. I'm sorry."

Susan seemed quick to forgive. She nuzzled Katie's shoulder through the insulated coveralls. "Next time I'll bring you a goodie, I promise. I was just a little distracted this morning. Any woman would have been if she woke up with a gorgeous man in her kitchen—even a bossy, annoying one like Peter Logan."

Susan snorted and it sounded so much like the horse agreed with her that Katie couldn't help laughing.

Just as abruptly, her laughter faded. To her considerable dismay, she found herself sobbing instead. For the first time since discovering she was pregnant, Katie gave in to the jumbled emotions raging through her—anxiety and fear and dismay and joy.

Susan nickered and nudged her shoulder again, as if she wanted to give comfort, and Katie buried her face in the horse's warm neck. Where was all this emotion coming from? she wondered. It sneaked up on her out of nowhere, and she didn't know how to cope with it.

Not that she was ever much good at handling emotions, Katie thought. She had spent so much of her childhood trying to stay out of trouble that she suppressed the natural highs and lows every child learns to contend with. After her engagement ended so disastrously, she finally forced herself to see a therapist. Dr. Sikes helped her figure out that she turned to food to avoid facing the thick soup of emotions simmering inside her—the rage and rejection and loneliness.

Talking things out had helped her finally break the vicious cycle between what she ate and how she felt. It had worked with Dr. Sikes and maybe it would help her now.

Though she felt a little silly, she found herself now spilling the whole story of Peter and the charity gala to Susan, who listened with wide, compassionate eyes and only gave the occasional snort in response.

Ten minutes later she felt much better. She wiped at her eyes with the heavy sleeve of her coveralls, grateful beyond measure that Peter was tending to the cattle and hadn't caught her.

Though she knew it wasn't healthy to suppress her emotions completely, she also knew she couldn't afford to give in to them right now. Not with Peter here at Sweetwater, watching her every move. She couldn't give him any hint that she was pregnant. If he found out, he would be livid.

She had to be strong, as stoic as Clint, until Peter left for Portland and she could figure out how to go on from here.

There was no question she was keeping her child. She loved her already, the tiny little life growing inside her. She didn't know how she could so fiercely love someone she hadn't known existed a week ago but she did know she was going to work hard to be a good mother.

Her own childhood had been terribly unhealthy, between Sheila's complete self-absorption and Jack's workaholic disinterest. But Katie was going to do everything in her power to give her own daughter a wonderful future, where her baby knew every moment of her life that she was loved.

That happy picture certainly didn't include Peter Logan. It couldn't possibly.

The wind still shrieked and howled when Peter finished with the cattle and returned to the barn. The two low-slung dogs led the way, leaping through snow drifts about as high as they were.

His muscles ached from the exertion of forking

hay bales and fighting the storm, but he didn't mind. It was a pleasant kind of burn, the ache of knowing he had worked hard and earned each twinge.

He wasn't out of shape; he believed a tight, well-functioning body helped his mind work harder. He swam several dozen laps and ruthlessly lifted weights each morning. This was a different ache, though, one of knowing he had accomplished something more worthwhile than making it to the end of the pool in record time.

He caught the direction of his thoughts and gave a rueful laugh. If he wasn't careful, he might find himself tempted to buy a ranch and move west. No, thanks. He would stick with his weights and his lap pool. His usual workout might lack this noble sense of purpose, but at least when he was done he could usually feel his toes and his eyelashes didn't freeze together.

Just in the hour or so since he'd left, more snow had piled up in front of the barn door and he had to shovel it away to swing the door open. The dogs were as eager as he for the warmth of the barn. They sidled through and immediately found their cozy spot.

He found Katherine nose to nose with one of the horses. She was still wearing her insulated coveralls but had removed her hat and her hair stuck out in little spikes.

"How did it go with the cattle?" she asked.

"Good. Your foreman runs a tight ship. Everything was right where he said it would be. I only had to fork the bales over the fence and the cattle came running."

"What about water?"

"There were a few spots of ice in the middle of the tank but the cattle seemed to be able to get enough water around the edges."

She frowned. "You said you saw some patches of ice? That's not right. The warmer should keep the water above freezing so there isn't any ice. Clint said he was a little concerned with that unit. I wonder if it's malfunctioning."

"They were still able to get to the water."

"Keeping a good water supply is vital to the cattle all year long but especially in winter. We'll have to keep an eye on it. It's solar powered but has a battery backup that should keep it juiced up even during the cloudiest of days."

She stepped away from the horse and he had his first full-on look at her since he had returned to the barn. Her eyes looked puffy and her nose was red.

"Is everything all right in here?"

She tilted her chin, a belligerent look in her eyes. "Just fine. Why wouldn't it be?"

He couldn't just come out and say she looked as if she'd been crying. In his experience, women didn't always appreciate that kind of information.

Besides, if she had been crying—something he

found hard to reconcile with the sneaky manipulator he had decided she must be—he wasn't sure he wanted to know. It made her too human, too vulnerable.

Had he come on too strong before, bossing her around as he had? Too bad, he thought. He meant every word and would have had no compunction about locking her in the tack room while he cared for the stock.

If she was crying, it was probably because she hated being beholden to a Logan. Rather than go down that dangerous road—or any road that involved a woman's tears—he opted to change the subject.

"Nice horse. Is she yours?"

Katie gave him an odd look but seemed willing enough to travel the conversational side route. "Yes. Her name is Susan."

"And does Susan ever answer during your conversations?"

She flushed so brightly he had to wonder what she had been talking to the horse about. "No. That's why she's such a perfect conversationalist. Unlike some people," she added pointedly, "Susan doesn't pick at me or make unfounded accusations or call me names. All she does is snort once in a while."

"What's the fun of that?"

If he didn't know better, he would have thought there was a smile lurking in her eyes, but she didn't allow it anywhere near her mouth. "Does your family have horses?"

"No. I've ridden a few times but I would probably fall into the tenderfoot category. I suppose you grew up riding."

Her laugh was brief and humorless. "No. Sheila hates horses, unless she's watching them on the race-track. She dislikes animals of all kinds. We weren't allowed any pets."

That didn't surprise him at all. He knew the grim history between their families well enough to hold Sheila Crosby responsible for much of the pain his parents had endured at the loss of their oldest son. Robbie supposedly had been under her supervision at the time of his kidnapping. Even after she realized he had disappeared, she had been too busy covering her own rear end to help the investigation.

He despised the matriarch of the Crosby clan. In his opinion she was selfish and amoral, interested only in herself.

"But you ride now?" he asked Sheila's daughter.

"I didn't learn until I was sent to Switzerland and boarding school. All the other girls seemed to have been born in the saddle. They couldn't understand how anybody could be as graceless and uncoordi-nated as I was at it. I was terrified of the horses and was forever falling off."

Girls could be cruel to each other—especially spoiled rich girls at Swiss boarding schools, he imagined.

"You must have stuck with it or you wouldn't be here talking to Susan, the great conversationalist."

She smiled suddenly and Peter was startled at how just that small change in her expression could make her look so young.

"The first year I was away from home I spent every afternoon at the riding stables until I was able to overcome my fear of the horses. The riding master and the grooms were just about the only friends I had for a long time. I'm sure they were sick of me, but they were very patient."

He didn't like the image that had suddenly formed in his mind, of a younger version of this woman haunting the stables at her school until she could overcome her fear.

"How old were you when you went to boarding school?"

"Eleven."

What had her parents been thinking to send her away at such a tender age? His dislike for Sheila Crosby intensified. Everything he'd seen about the woman showed him she treated her children with casual disinterest, except when she wanted something from them.

"Tough age," he murmured.

"I survived. The horses helped."

How much pain and loneliness did those mild words conceal? he wondered.

Being away at such a formative time in a young girl's life must have been terribly lonely, especially if she hadn't fit in at her boarding school.

He thought of his own sisters, Bridget and Jillian. His mother never would have let them leave the house so young. She would have shriveled up and died without them. But Sheila Crosby was a far different woman than Leslie Logan.

On the other hand, with Sheila for a mother, maybe boarding school hadn't been such a bad thing.

He didn't like the compassion flickering through him. Why should he care if she had a lonely childhood? That didn't excuse the kind of woman she had become, one who could lie about her name and sleep with a business rival to pry out company secrets.

He didn't care, he told himself. He only wanted to find out more about her. Know thine enemy and all that.

"How long were you at boarding school?"

"Five years. I was admitted early to Stanford when I was sixteen and graduated with my masters at twenty-one. I've been at Crosby ever since."

"I understand your sister, Ivy, worked there, too, until her marriage to that Lantanyan royal."

"Yes. I talked her into coming to Crosby after the dot-com she worked for went bust. That's how she met Max," Katie went on. "She was in Lantanya managing the installation of one of our high-speed computer systems to link all their schools."

Her eyes lit up when she talked about her siblings, Peter thought. He wondered if she knew it.

She talked about her siblings with the same pride he talked about Eric and David and Jillian and Bridget.

He didn't like thinking they had this in common. It was far easier to dislike the whole Crosby clan when he viewed them as a bed of vipers, each willing to strike out at the other.

"Trent must have hated to lose another potential spy in his little network," he said, then instantly regretted the comment. It was petty and mean and all but extinguished that light in her eyes.

"Right. Technically, Ivy's staying on at Crosby to oversee the Lantanya project. But since she's busy with a new husband, her royal responsibilities and a baby on the way, she probably won't have time for much corporate espionage. I guess that means Trent is stuck with only me to do his dirty work."

"Well, you're good at what you do."

"If I need references for my next assignment, I'll be sure to come to you," she snapped.

He opened his mouth to snap back a retort, but before he could, the horse whinnied and shoved her nose into Katie's back, almost as if she didn't like her suddenly sharp tone.

Katie stumbled a little and would have fallen, but Peter instinctively stepped forward and caught her against him.

She was curvy and warm in his arms, a perfect fit, and like a match set to dry tinder, his body immediately reacted to her nearness just as it had done the night of the gala, as if three months and a world of bitterness didn't exist between them.

He would have released her as soon as she found her footing again but then she looked at him. An odd expression flitted across those huge, gorgeous brown eyes. He couldn't sort out all the emotions there, but if he didn't know better, he might have believed he saw longing and regret there.

He still wanted her. He didn't like it, but his body still yearned for her, still ached to touch her skin and kiss her mouth and fill his senses with her. Knowing she shared his hunger didn't make things any easier.

He had to kiss her. Just one kiss to see if the fire and intensity between them that night had been a fluke. He leaned forward, but just before his mouth met hers, he saw something else flare in her eyes, something that almost looked like fear.

What was she afraid of? Him? Impossible! Okay, maybe he'd groused and yelled a little since he showed up at Sweetwater. He might have come on a bit overbearing with that whole locking her in the tack room bit but she had to know he would never hurt a woman, even a Crosby.

Despite what she had done to him, the irreparable harm she may have caused to his family and his position as CEO, he hated the idea that she might be afraid of him.

"Katie—"

He wasn't sure what he was going to say but she didn't give him a chance to finish the sentence. She jerked out of his arms and backed away until she almost hit the stall's wooden railing.

"Since the animals are fed and watered, there's no reason to hang around here. I'm going back to the house."

Before he could argue, she rushed out of the barn, leaving him with the odd feeling that something significant had just happened between them—if he could only figure out what.

Six

"Will this damn storm ever stop?"

Katie glanced up from the mystery novel she had been pretending to read toward the spot where Peter stood at the wide picture window of the room, his fingers curled around the windowsill as he glowered out at the unrelenting snow.

"It can't snow forever," she murmured. "Spring eventually comes, even here in Wyoming."

"Very funny. I don't particularly care to be trapped here until the vernal equinox, thanks very much."

Every inch of him radiated tension, from the stiff set of his shoulders to the taut muscles of his jawline, and she regretted baiting him.

Peter Logan was obviously a man unused to inactivity. Since they had returned to the house from caring for the animals, he had been restless and edgy.

Of course, she hadn't been exactly serene, she admitted. After that scene in the barn when they had bickered and he had nearly kissed her, she had rushed back to the house, barely noticing the snowdrifts she struggled through. She hadn't even minded the relentless wind that whipped icy air and snow in a vicious mix. At least the cold helped cool her cheeks and her overheated senses.

How could she be foolish enough to crave his touch after everything between them? He despised her. She knew he did and yet she still hungered for him.

What a disaster it would have been if he had kissed her. She had been so afraid he would, terrified that she would respond to him as she had the night of the benefit and that his kiss would lead to more.

If she slept with him again, she wouldn't be able to keep the truth about the baby to herself. She would have told him everything, which would have been an unmitigated disaster.

Nothing happened, though. He had stopped just before he would have kissed her. She was glad, she told herself. That ache in her heart had only been the exertion of fighting the storm.

By the time she reached the house, she had her emotions firmly in control. He followed her a few moments later and she forced herself to pretend that scene in the barn never happened.

He seemed just as eager to forget it. While she reheated stew for their lunch, Peter took out a laptop from the luggage he'd retrieved out of his rental Jeep the night before and began working feverishly on it, his brow furrowed with concentration.

She had thought about retreating to her bedroom but it seemed foolish and wasteful to keep two fires going just because of her own cowardice. The great room was large enough that they surely could both inhabit it without gnawing at each other's throats, so she had forced herself to curl up on a couch and pretend to read.

She should enjoy the chance to put her feet up for a few moments while she was temporarily nausea-free, she tried to tell herself.

After a few hours of activity at the computer during which he had picked up the phone at least a half-dozen times looking for a dial tone, only to slam it down with disgust when he remembered the phone was out, Peter must have finished as much as he could. He snapped the laptop shut and stalked to the window, where he had spent the last fifteen minutes glaring out at the storm beyond.

She was the hostess here, despite the fact that the role had been thrust on her against her will. She should at least try to alleviate his boredom.

"I'm sure the generator's got enough power that

you could watch something on TV," she offered. "There's quite an extensive DVD collection. Everything from comedies to action-adventure to Westerns."

"I'm not much for movies or television. I like to watch a little basketball but that's about it."

"The ranch has a satellite system. You might have to sweep the snow out of the dish but you could probably find a game on."

"No, thanks."

"We could play a board game or something. Chess, cards, Monopoly. You probably love that one."

That idea obviously didn't appeal to him, either, judging by the surly look he sent her, so Katie figuratively threw up her hands. "Or you can keep pacing around the room like a caged grizzly. It's all the same to me. Stirring up all those molecules in the air must be helping the room stay a little warmer, at any rate."

Perversely, her annoyance seemed to cheer him up. He smiled and returned to the couch. "Getting on your nerves, am I?"

"You're not the most restful of companions." *In more ways than one,* she wanted to add, but swallowed the words.

"Sorry. My brother, Eric, in his more lyrical moments used to complain that I've got more energy than a one-armed monkey at a flea festival."

She laughed at the image. "My brother, Trent, is the same way. He always has to be busy doing something. I suppose it must be part of the whole CEO package."

He didn't look thrilled at the comparison to her brother, but Katie refused to feel guilty for bringing up what was obviously a touchy subject. She loved her brother dearly and wouldn't allow Peter's irrational dislike to prevent her from even bringing up Trent's name.

She waited for some kind of snide comment from him about Trent but he let the subject drop. Maybe he wanted a ceasefire as much as she did. She studied him, wondering about this complex, perplexing man who would give their child half its DNA.

What kind of a child had he been? she wondered. Had he been obedient or rebellious? Extroverted or withdrawn? She knew he had been a good student and she knew he could have moments of deep kindness but she suddenly wanted to know more.

Since they had nothing else to do, maybe they could manage to set aside their differences and have a real conversation, just so she could gain some insights into his personality. Maybe if she knew a little more about him, she could get some idea what traits he might pass on to their child.

"You're the oldest child, right?"

"The oldest *living* child," he said sharply.

Robbie again, she remembered, with her customary pang of sympathy for the Logans. As tragic as Robbie's kidnapping and death had been, she never forgot that although they had lost a son, in a very real way she had lost a brother that day, too. Danny had never stopped blaming himself for his best friend's disappearance, for not protecting him somehow.

Over the years, that guilt had manifested itself in horrible ways. In his teens, Danny had sought release in drugs and alcohol but had since turned his life around.

After he married, she thought maybe at last he could be happy. But that, too, had ended tragically when history grimly repeated itself and Danny's own son was kidnapped from a city park. His wife had been unable to bear the pain of losing her child and had killed herself, and Danny had retreated to his private island off the coast of Hawaii. No one seemed able to reach him. She tried as best she could but he was lost in his own hell outside her understanding.

Although she had visited him a few times, he seemed to prefer his solitude.

"Do you get along with your siblings?" she asked Peter.

He looked surprised at the question but finally nodded. "We're a very close family."

"There are five of you, right?"

"Right. I'm the oldest, then the twins, although my parents didn't adopt them until they were five, after they'd had Eric and Bridget."

"That's right. I'd forgotten David and Jillian were adopted, too."

"Right."

"You were six when you were adopted by the Logans, weren't you? Do you remember anything of your life before you went to live with them?"

The sudden chill in his eyes at her question was far colder than anything Mother Nature could dish out. Despite the merry warmth from the fire, she shivered. Apparently she had crossed some intangible line by asking about his childhood. She wished she could yank back the question, but the words were already out there, hovering in the air.

"Forget I asked. I was simply making conversation but I can see now it was a presumptuous question. I apologize."

He was quiet for a moment longer, the silence broken only by the flames snapping in the hearth.

"I remember a little," he finally answered. "Not much of it good. I remember washing up in a dirty bus station sink once and sleeping at a shelter with some other kids. A bigger kid stole my toy airplane so I belted him. The woman who gave birth to me—I don't consider her my mother—was a heroin addict and a prostitute. She couldn't even take care of herself, forget about seeing to the needs of a kid. We were lucky to have a roof over our heads most nights."

Her heart twisted with sorrow for the little boy he must have been. Tears burned behind her eyelids and though she knew perfectly well he wouldn't welcome the gesture, she fought the urge to draw him against her for comfort.

"And your father?" she asked, then hoped he didn't notice the rough note in her voice.

"Don't know. I doubt she did, either." He shrugged. "I don't think about it much anymore. In every way that matters, my father is Terrence Logan and my mother is Leslie Logan."

"You were happy with them?"

"The day they adopted me from Children's Connection was the best day of my life. My first good memory is riding home with them from the orphanage, sitting wedged between them in the front seat of the car and feeling safe and warm for the first time in my life. I vowed that day that I would never do anything to disappoint them or make them regret picking me out of all the other kids at the orphanage."

Was that why he was so driven to succeed? she wondered. Why he was known as a completely focused, brilliant executive? When Terrence Logan retired, one of the Portland newspapers ran a big story about Peter taking over. She had always been fascinated with him and had read it with far more interest than she liked to admit.

In the story, she learned he had worked harder than she to get where he was. He was valedictorian of the exclusive private prep school he attended and also graduated magna cum laude from the Harvard School of Business. Like her, he had gone to work at his family's company right after graduation.

Where she preferred working behind the scenes in

research and development, he seemed to have no problem being in the limelight. Through his tenure at Logan, Peter had earned a reputation in the Portland business community as a fiercely loyal, dedicated, passionate CEO who gave everything to his work.

Was his dedication to the firm and his passion for the job just another way he tried to prove to Leslie and Terrence they hadn't made a mistake in adopting him?

She had a feeling he would deny it vigorously if she asked but something told her she was on the right track.

"I'm sure they're very proud of you," she said quietly. "You've been a good son to them."

"I've tried. I'm sure they've been disappointed in me a few times but they've always loved me anyway."

Would Terrence and Leslie be heartbroken if they ever found out Peter had fathered a grandchild they would never know? The thought jolted her. She had been thinking all along of the ramifications of keeping her pregnancy a secret from Peter but she hadn't given a thought to the concentric circle of people who would be affected by her decision.

By keeping the information from him, she suddenly realized she would also be depriving his family of the chance to know his child—and her child the chance to know his or her birthright.

She couldn't change her mind now, Katie thought. Though she might better understand Peter's single-minded passion to succeed now, that certainly didn't ameliorate it, by any means. She had grown up with a father who had the same focus, who saw nothing beyond his ambition and his ego and the women who fed it.

Peter Logan was too much like Jack Crosby for her to ever consider him good father material, though she knew he would rather wander naked out into that subzero storm than ever concede he might have anything in common with her father.

She wished suddenly that she'd never asked him about his childhood. She didn't want to picture a six-year-old boy with dark hair and brown eyes and a sweet smile vowing never to disappoint his new family. She also didn't need this guilt pinching at her when she thought of depriving Leslie and Terrence—who had lost so much already because of her family—the chance to know their grandchild.

She especially didn't want to feel this wary tenderness entwining around her heart.

Peter hadn't meant to tell her that whole bit about the day the Logans took him home. He never talked about it—hell, he didn't even think about it much. He meant what he'd said to her. In every way that mattered Terrence and Leslie were his parents. He loved them fiercely and never let himself forget how much he owed them.

He couldn't imagine how his life would have turned out if they hadn't adopted him. If he hadn't died early from malnutrition or one of the other many dangers he faced living on the street with a junkie and a whore for a mother, he didn't doubt that he would have spent his entire childhood either in the Children's Connection orphanage or in the foster-care system as a ward of the state.

Everything he had, all he had become, he owed to Leslie and Terrence, and he refused to lose sight of that.

They had never treated him any differently than their other children. They showered all of them—Eric and Bridget, their natural-born, and the adopted twins David and Jillian—with the same steady love and attention. But even when he'd been just a kid, Peter had always been conscious of the debt he owed them.

While other teenage boys were experimenting with alcohol or trying to score with the head cheerleader, he was knuckling down at his studies or following his father around, trying to learn the ropes at Logan.

As he'd said to Katie, he knew there had been times he had been a disappointment to them, but overall he knew they were proud of the man he'd become.

That all might change, though. He didn't think they would be too crazy about the idea that he was here, trapped on a ranch with Katie Crosby—or about the circumstances that had led him here.

After all the bitterness between their families, he didn't want to think about how disappointed Leslie and Terrence would be when they saw that article in the *Weekly* and when they learned he may have compromised an important project because of his lust.

He had a feeling they also wouldn't be real thrilled to know how much he still burned for this particular Crosby.

Why was he so attracted to her? he wondered. He shouldn't be. She wasn't at all his usual type. She wasn't wearing makeup and her short, choppy hair was tousled. She still had circles under her eyes and she wore a baggy sweater, a pair of old jeans with frayed cuffs and thick wool socks the color of dryer lint.

But still he wanted her. All he could think about was the tight, lithe body underneath her clothes and the way she had responded in his arms with such fire and heat.

There was the real reason for his restlessness. Whenever he tried to concentrate on the shareholders report, all he could think about was how different things could have been between him and Katie.

If he never learned who she was—if he still thought she was the incredible, passionate Celeste—he would have given his left arm to find himself snowbound here alone with her.

He could have come up with at least a dozen ways to make love to her in every corner of this sprawling ranch house. Instead of this restless tension between them, they could be cuddling together under thick quilts, listening to the wind moan under the rafters and the snow tap against the glass. Or they could have curled up together in front of the fireplace with a bottle of wine.

The possibilities were limited only by his imagination and his stamina, and he had a feeling when it came to Katie Crosby he would have more than enough of both.

His body was only too willing to forget how angry he was about this whole mess, about her lies and even about her identity. His mind refused to capitulate, though.

It didn't help that he found her even more desirable here under these primitive conditions than with all the glitz and glamour of the charity benefit. She seemed more comfortable here, more natural.

Except for that moment in the barn when she had run away from him, she didn't even seem to mind his company.

"Why are you staring?" she asked him suddenly. His gaze met hers before he had a chance to mask the desire he knew was only too evident there. To his surprise, a blush crept from her throat to her cheekbones.

He didn't begin to understand this woman. He didn't understand most women—he'd be the first to admit it. He enjoyed women, figured it was safe to say he loved everything about them. The way they smelled, the fancy things they did to their hair, the way they seemed incapable of visiting the ladies' room unless they went as a pack.

His brother, Eric, was the expert, the one who always knew just what to say and how to smile and where to touch. Eric had been charming women from the cradle.

To Peter, all women were a tantalizing, delicious mystery. But this one in particular had him baffled. How could she seduce him with such calculating cold-bloodedness, yet still blush at a look in his eyes?

It didn't make sense. *She* didn't make sense. He knew she slept with him that night to spy on their super-router project. Why else would she have lied to him about who she was, have kissed him on the balcony of Dorothea's hotel room and then again so eagerly in the limousine? Why would she have even climbed into that limo with him if she hadn't been planning all along to seduce him into taking her home?

Here, Katie seemed completely different. Softer, less sophisticated, maybe. She was someone he almost thought he could like under other circumstances.

"Peter?"

How long had he been staring at her with hunger in his eyes, he wondered, annoyed at himself.

"Why didn't you tell me who you were?" he asked suddenly and rose to his feet.

Her eyes widened at the question. As if she didn't like being at a height disadvantage, she rose, too, and stuck out that stubborn little chin. "I thought you already figured that out. It was all part of my devious plan. Isn't that what you think? You never would have slept with me if you had known I was Katherine Crosby."

"I'm not so sure of that," he muttered in a voice that should have been too low for her to hear.

She must have uncommonly good hearing, though. She stared at him. "What did you say?"

It was too late to back down, even if he wanted to. "I know exactly who you are now. So explain to me how I can still want you."

His words seemed to echo in the vast room. He would have let the matter drop, just left his imprudent admission to hover there between them, but he saw her pupils flare and saw her chest rise and fall in quick succession with her gasp.

Though he knew he would likely hate himself for it later, he couldn't resist tasting her, just one more time. Only once, he promised himself as he lowered his mouth to hers. Just a taste and then he would retreat back into his anger.

He could swear he felt the slow churn of blood through his veins and each rapid beat of his heart as he lowered his mouth to hers, swallowing another quick intake of her breath as their lips met.

Her mouth was soft, warm and just as delicious as he remembered. He wanted to taste every inch of it, to lick and probe and savor until she forgot even her own name.

Or at least until he forgot it.

He had missed this, the low burn of desire in his

gut. He hadn't been with a woman since their night together three months ago. He hadn't even dated anyone, hadn't even been tempted to go out.

Even on New Year's Eve, he had gone alone to a party at a friend's house rather than summon the energy to ask anyone out when all he could think about was Celeste.

And here she was in his arms again, just as he had imagined hundreds of times, before he found out who she was. She fit against him just as perfectly as she had that night. Her body was curvy in all the right places. After that first moment when she stood motionless in his arms as though paralyzed by shock, her arms wrapped around him and she leaned into him. Her mouth softened under his and everything about her seemed to sigh.

He wanted to fill his senses with her. She smelled the same as she had that night, some kind of subtle floral scent that made him think of his mother's garden after an April rain.

He didn't know how long they kissed. He only knew he would have been happy to stand just like this for a week or two, with the wind howling at the window and the fire snapping in the grate. But when he lowered a hand to the small of her back to draw her closer, she seemed to snap back to her senses. Her eyes jerked open and she dropped her arms from around his neck and scrambled away as if she'd just found herself embracing a python.

If her uneven breathing was any indication, their embrace affected her as intensely as it did him. "What was that all about?" she asked, her voice thin, ragged.

"Isn't it obvious?"

She was quiet for a moment, then she shook her head. "You're bored and restless. Inactivity is diffi-cult for a man like you. I understand that and I'm sorry for it, but I won't help you pass the time this way. I *won't*. Not when it's obvious you despise me."

"I don't despise you."

Her laugh was harsh and disbelieving. "Right."

Why so much bitterness? he wondered. Her eyes were as bleak as the landscape outside the window.

"I don't."

It was the truth, he was startled to discover, but she didn't appear at all convinced. "I'm going to check on the fuel level on the generator and then see what I can round up for dinner."

And don't bother coming with me. She didn't add the words but he heard them loud and clear.

Seven

The storm broke a few hours before dawn.

Though Katie should have been sleeping, oblivious to any change in weather at that ungodly hour, she had been lying awake in bed, the quilt snug around her chin as she gazed at the dying flames' sinuous dance and replayed their kiss.

She couldn't figure out why Peter had done it. He had seemed genuinely shocked when she accused him of merely trying to pass the time, kissing her out of boredom and restlessness.

But what other reason could there be?

He didn't like her and certainly didn't trust her. He had made that abundantly clear since he arrived at

Sweetwater. He thought she had slept with him only to learn Logan Corporation secrets. So why kiss her until her bones melted? Until she was moaning and panting and closer than she cared to remember to begging for more?

She knew how dangerous it was to kiss him. Between her pregnancy and the trauma of seeing him again, her emotions were fragile, weak. She didn't like feeling vulnerable and exposed. She needed time and space to build her defenses against him but she'd had neither since his arrival.

Had it only been a day and a half? She couldn't believe it. Time seemed to stretch and thin. She felt as if she'd lived a lifetime in those thirty-six hours. Maybe because they had been together almost constantly since he swept into Sweetwater.

Even after that kiss, when she had wanted desperately to retreat to her room and hide away, she had forced herself to remain either in the kitchen or the great room.

After the dinner she had put together—well, the lasagna she had pulled out of the freezer and baked according to Margie's directions—she had even gone so far as to play a game with him. Monopoly. No big surprise, he won. She wasn't any better at empire building, she decided, than she was at forgetting how she had wanted to let him hold her forever.

Why had he kissed her? She had been up most of the night trying to figure it out but had come no closer to a solution when she suddenly registered a strange silence. It took her a moment to realize the mournful keening of the wind had stopped at last, leaving behind an unearthly quiet. She slipped from the bed and padded to the window.

The clouds had finally shifted and moonlight gleamed on the tiny fluttery snowflakes drifting slowly down. She found it hard to believe that the violence and rage of the storm could blow itself out and leave this tranquil scene, everything white-blue and still.

She watched it for a long time, trying to absorb some of that calm into her own psyche.

With the storm dying out, she knew Peter wouldn't be at Sweetwater much longer. It would probably take another day or so for the roads to be cleared and then he would be able to fly back to Portland.

She should be relieved, especially with the unbearable tension of the last evening after their kiss. When he was gone, she could at last find at the ranch what she had come for—peace.

She knew she should be praying for the roads to be cleared quickly so he could leave and she could come to terms with the changes her life was about to undergo.

But here in the quiet of her room in those grim hours before dawn, she could admit the truth. Her heart ached with a deep sense of loss whenever she thought about him returning to Portland. He would return to his world and she to hers. They might see each other at the rare social occasion but he would be cold and formal and distant.

She sighed as depression settled heavily on her shoulders. The wood floor was cold against her toes and she couldn't stifle a yawn. She knew she needed to sleep. She didn't know much about being pregnant except that pregnant women needed plenty of rest for the hard work of nurturing tiny developing bodies.

She threw another log on the fire then crawled into bed again, grateful her spot was still warm. After she pulled the quilt up to her chin, she pressed a hand to her abdomen.

"Good night," she whispered.

At least she didn't feel *completely* alone.

Hours later, Katie yawned, feeling the effects of too little sleep. She had managed three or four hours but they weren't nearly enough. If not for the cold whipping through her, keeping her senses as sharp as possible, she was afraid she would fall asleep in the saddle.

From atop Susan, the snow looked brilliant, so white her eyes burned even behind the sunglasses she had unearthed out of her luggage.

"How are you doing over there?" she called to Peter, riding next to her on a big roan gelding.

"Surprisingly well. And here I thought those riding lessons at Boy Scout camp twenty years ago would never come in handy."

She smiled at his wry tone. "You're doing great."

"Well, I haven't fallen off so I guess that's saying something."

With Luke and Millie following the horses' trail, Katie nudged Susan and the pack horse she led forward, following the fenceline around a copse of evergreen trees whose fringy branches sagged under the weight of the snow. The fence had acted as a windbreak, effectively containing much of the blowing snow behind posts wearing brilliant white top hats.

Though the horses still had to work hard to plunge through the deep snow, it wasn't anywhere near as high as the drifts on the other side of the fence.

She hoped this wasn't another fool's errand. After checking the huge round water trough closest to the barn while feeding the animals earlier, Peter had discovered the warmer she'd been worried about the day before had completely gone out sometime during the night, leaving a four-inch layer of ice.

They had managed to break it up with shovels and pitchforks but Katie knew with these frigid temperatures, she and Peter would have to come out several times a day and smash new ice as it formed unless they could figure something else out.

The cattle could eat snow for some of their necessary water but it wouldn't be enough, not with this cold.

There was an identical watering system on the distant side of the two-hundred-acre pasture and Katie had come up with the grand idea of switching its warmer with the broken unit until Clint returned and could figure out what had gone haywire.

She could have retrieved it by herself but Peter insisted on coming along. Probably afraid to let her out of his sight, she thought grumpily, just in case she had nefarious plans to slip more Logan Corporation secrets to someone in her vast and intricate spy network.

But if he thought she was some kind of evil corporate spy, why did he kiss her?

She was no closer to figuring that out than she'd been at 4:00 a.m. Her sigh fogged the air, even through her thick muffler.

"Everything okay?" he asked.

Peachy. Just peachy. I'm pregnant and exhausted and queasy and can't say a word about any of it. "There's the water tank." She changed the subject. "And look, no ice. At least something's working."

They both dismounted and hitched their horses to the fence keeping the cattle away from a small storage shed near the watering station.

"Since this one has plenty of water, why can't the cattle just drink from here?" Peter asked as they walked to the tank.

"All the cattle have been sticking close to the barn since that's where they catch the gravy train. If we make them trudge all the way out here to drink, I'm afraid they'll burn up so many calories we'll have to put out even more feed to keep them warm enough. The colder the temperature, the more food the cattle need. Add this kind of extra exercise even for a few days and either they'll start losing bulk or the ranch will have to dig into its overhead to cover the cost of feed."

His mouth twisted into a half smile as he studied her. "I never would have taken Katherine Crosby for a cowgirl."

"I'm just full of surprises, aren't I?"

"I'm beginning to think so."

What did he mean by that? she wondered. She could feel a blush heat her skin and cleared her throat, unnerved by a strange light in his eyes. "We'd better figure this out so we can get out of the cold."

Like the one closer to the barn, the warming unit was solar powered and it took her a few moments to figure out how to take it apart. Give her a computer CPU and she could have it apart and back together in the blink of an eye, but cattle trough warming units weren't exactly in her line of expertise. Finally she managed to disconnect it from the solar cells.

Peter reached to take the floating unit from her. He carried it back to the trio of horses and helped her tie it down on the back of the pack horse.

"Is that it?" Peter asked. "Are we done here?"

"I think so—" she started to say, but her words were cut off by a whoosh as a deep shelf of snow slid off the steep roof of the storage shed—and directly onto Peter, standing below. Only his head was left sticking out of the pile of snow.

"Are you all right?" she gasped, rushing forward to help him.

"Dandy," he muttered. She could tell by his tone that he wasn't hurt, only disgruntled at being buried. In her relief, she finally took time to really look at him. The sight made her stop in her tracks and cover her mouth with a gloved hand, but she was too late to stop a giggle.

Oh, how she wished that dratted *Portland Weekly* photographer were here now! She would love a picture of the oh-so-correct Peter Logan standing in the middle of a cattle pasture like the abominable snowman, with snow covering him from head to toe.

"It's not funny," he growled. He shook his head vigorously, flinging snow in every direction.

"Oh, it is. I'm sorry, but if you could see yourself right now, you'd be laughing, too."

He glared at her. "I'm blaming you for this, Ms. Crosby. I should be safe and warm and hard at work in Portland right now. I left a million things undone, every single one of them far more important than rolling around in snow and cow manure, fixing your stupid trough warmer."

"I'm sorry," she said again, then laughed even harder at his offended dignity. Soon she was whooping uncontrollably. Every time she thought she had it contained he would dig himself out a little farther, pausing just long enough to send another glare her way, and she would start again.

He must think she was insane, she thought. If someone had laughed at her in the same situation, she likely would have been livid.

Though one corner of her mind knew she ought to be helping him, she couldn't seem to do anything but stand in the snow and laugh like some half-crazy hyena.

Maybe it was her lack of sleep or maybe the stress she'd been living with. But it felt wonderful to let go and laugh. She didn't want to stop.

If he could have kept his eyes off Katie, Peter might have been able to dig himself out and clear the snow off various parts of his person much faster. But even as the cold snow started to permeate his heavy clothing, he couldn't manage to look away.

She was so beautiful she took his breath away. She glowed out here. With her cheeks rosy and her nose pink from the cold, she shined brighter than the brilliant Wyoming sunshine glittering off the snow. He had never seen this side of her. She didn't look sophisticated or glamorous or even cool and remote as she'd been since he came to the ranch.

Out here, Katie looked young and lighthearted, and he was helpless to resist that infectious laugh.

"I guess I should probably help you," she gasped out between peals of laughter.

"Oh, don't mind me. I have no problem staying here until the snow melts."

That set her off again but she hurried over, still

laughing, and began to scoop away the snow mound surrounding him.

"Here," she said after several moments of digging. "Let's see if I can tug you out of the rest of it now."

She gripped his hands and pulled with all her might. He felt his snowy cage give way and with the added force, he was able to pull his boots free and climb out.

All would have been well, but when Katie let go of his hands, the momentum of her tug carried her backward and with an "oomph" she landed on her rear end in the snow.

Under other circumstances, he would have hurried to help her up. But since she had found such unbridled amusement a few moments earlier at his expense, he found he couldn't resist taking whatever advantage he could find. He scooped up a huge armload of snow and with complete, ungentlemanly satisfaction, dumped it on her head.

She shrieked and sputtered, then stared at him with snow dripping off her hat and down her coat.

"I can't believe you just did that."

Neither could he, truth be told. Leslie would have been appalled at him for picking on a girl. But he had to admit, revenge—no matter how petty—had felt pretty damn good.

He shrugged. "You're right. Wearing all that snow does look funny from this angle."

With the sleeve of her coat, she wiped the snow

off her face and her hat then narrowed her gaze at him. Her red nose spoiled the menace in her glare, as did the delight gleaming in her eyes.

"You know this means war, don't you, Logan?"

In one smooth motion, she scooped up a snowball then fired it straight at his chin with perfect aim. It splatted on his already freezing skin in an icy mess. Before he could even think about retaliating, she rushed around the other side of the shed.

"Oh, that's it," he said with menace in his voice. "You don't know who you're messing with."

She giggled again and peeked her head around the corner of the shed just long enough to throw a snowball that didn't even come close to hitting the mark.

"Ha. Missed me." He sounded like a third-grader on the playground but suddenly he didn't care. All his fury and stress of the last few days seemed to melt away in the pale sunshine.

Her next snowball hit him square on the chest, but he was ready for her. Before she could retreat to safety, he lobbed one back at her. It struck her collarbone with a satisfying plop and she shrieked and ducked her head.

For the next ten minutes they played like children in the snow, with the dogs barking around them and joining in the fun. He forgot about being CEO of a Fortune 500 company, forgot about the dignity and decorum he usually tried to achieve. All he could focus on was retaliation.

Had he ever engaged in a good old-fashioned snowball fight as a kid? He couldn't remember. He knew Terrence and Leslie had taken them all skiing several times to Mount Hood and they'd even spent a few vacations on the slopes of Utah, but he only remembered concentrating fiercely on trying to ski well enough to keep up with his father, not playing in the snow.

He couldn't remember the last time he enjoyed himself so much. Now it was even more fun because Katie wasn't afraid to talk smack, with a creativity that amazed him.

She insulted his aim. She laughed at his asymmetrical snowballs that usually fell apart before they could land anywhere. She ridiculed his sneak-attack strategy of skulking past the horses to try to surprise her around the other side of the shed—only to find her poised and waiting for him with a rapid volley.

She also had a wicked curve ball. His shots missed more often than not, but hers nearly always found their mark.

Finally he was laughing too hard to throw anymore. He pulled his hat off, stuck it on a stick and thrust it around the side of the shed. "Truce," he called out.

After a moment she peeked her head around, her gaze narrowed. "How do I know this isn't just a sneaky Logan trick, so I let down my guard just enough that you can hit me with a firestorm?"

He grinned at her. "I guess you'll just have to trust me."

She appeared to think it over, then she walked around the shed toward him. "Okay."

Now it was his turn to study her with suspicion. "Just like that? It can't be that easy."

She shrugged when she reached him. "My nose is frozen and whipping your wussy butt makes me hungry. I'm ready for lunch."

She looked so adorably cheeky that he laughed and tugged her hat down over her eyes. Then, before he could check the motion, he dipped his head and kissed her.

Despite the cold temperatures, her mouth was warm—incredibly, seductively warm—and more inviting than a blazing fire. As soon as he kissed her, he forgot the snow and the cold and the horses stamping and snorting to return to the barn. All he could think about was her.

"You taste so good," he murmured against her mouth. "I don't want to stop."

"We'll freeze to death."

"I'm not sure I'd mind."

At his low words, she seemed to relax even more. Entwining her arms around his neck, she kissed him back with an eagerness that made him instantly hard and aching.

He wanted to drag her back to the house and make love to her until neither of them could move. He wanted to touch her and taste her and come inside her while she cried out his name, just as she had done the night of the gala.

And he could do none of them.

He *would* do none of them.

Though it was just about the toughest thing he'd ever done, he wrenched his mouth away and rested his forehead against hers. All the reasons why he couldn't touch her rattled through his mind.

Didn't he ever learn? He had spent most of the night castigating himself for his weakness in kissing her the night before.

Frustrated desire sharpened his tone. "Why couldn't your name be Smith or Jones or Fletcher? Why did you have to be a damn Crosby?"

He hadn't meant to speak the words but they escaped to hover in the cold air like black, greasy crows.

With a harsh intake of breath, she jerked away from him, her eyes bruised and hurt. "I can't change who I am, Peter. And even if I could, I wouldn't. I love my family, warts and all."

His own hurt at being used by her prodded him on, urged him to slash and cut and make her bleed as he finally acknowledged he had bled when he learned of her betrayal.

"And you'll do anything for them, won't you? Even screw a Logan, just to help out the family business."

She paled as if he had slapped her. All the warmth and happiness that had lit up her face during their play in the snow leached away, leaving her icy cold, her eyes huge in her ashen face.

Without another word, she turned her back on him and yanked her horse's reins free of the fence, then mounted before he could even make his boots work to follow her.

I'm sorry. The words rang in his ears, over and over and over, but he refused to let them spill out.

"I'm sure you can find your way back. Just follow the fence line," she said, her voice cool and without inflection.

Susan took off with a canter. It wasn't until Katie and the horse were several hundred yards away that he realized she had left him to lead the pack horse with the tank warmer.

Even with pushing Susan much harder than was safe in the heavy snow, Katie didn't quite make it to the thick copse of trees before she finally gave in to the tears burning behind her eyelids.

They slid free, only to freeze instantly on her cheeks. How was it that she hadn't noticed the cold at all while she and Peter had been engaged in their fierce snowball battle but now she could think of nothing but how frozen she was, how her bones felt as brittle as new icicles?

Damn Peter Logan. *Damn* him.

How could he make her feel so warm and cherished one moment, then like a two-bit whore the next?

What did he want from her? He wanted to punish her for deceiving him. That much had been clear since he showed up at Sweetwater, all fire and fury. Were these sweet, sensual, torturous kisses just another form of punishment? Part of some exquisite revenge on his part?

He wanted to make her burn for him just as she had that night, make her think maybe they could somehow find some peace between them, and then slap her back down, again and again.

She couldn't bear it.

She was such a fool. His contempt shouldn't have the power to wound her so viciously. She knew it shouldn't and yet she couldn't deny the ache in her heart.

She sniffed and swiped at her eyes. She was coming to care for him entirely too much.

How could she have let things get to this point?

She had been halfway in love with him after that night and now she was afraid she had come too far to turn back.

No. She couldn't be in love with him. Just the thought horrified her. She would just use all her considerable powers of reason and intellect to convince herself otherwise. It was as simple as that.

He would go back to Portland, probably as early as the next day, and she would stay here at Sweetwater until she worked this ridiculous infatuation out of her system.

In her rush to put as much distance as possible between her and Peter, she was pushing Susan far too hard for conditions. She realized it suddenly and started to rein her in. But before the horse could slow her momentum, she stumbled over some thick brush hidden beneath the snow.

If she had been concentrating as she should have been, Katie might have been able to stay in the saddle. It was only a little stumble, after all. But she was distracted by her emotions.

Add to that her thick gloves that didn't grip the reins as well as usual and the bulky snow boots she wore in place of ropers and that little stumble was all it took for her to go flying off.

She came down hard on one leg, then lost her balance and collapsed face-first into the snow, and the breath left her in a whoosh.

Eight

For several long seconds Katie tried frantically to suck oxygen into lungs that suddenly refused to function after the force of her fall. She lay in the snow, her chest pounding and her head spinning.

Oh, she hurt. She started to take an inventory of what pained her the most but gave up the overwhelming task. Despite the snow that cushioned her fall, every inch of her body complained loudly.

She wanted to curl up right here and just close her eyes for a moment, just long enough for the pain to subside and for her breathing to return to normal, but she knew she couldn't.

She had to force herself to move, not only because she didn't particularly care to freeze to death out here in the middle of nowhere, but also because she wasn't about to let Peter find her like this, bruised and shaken on the ground.

Susan nudged at her, her breath warm and her big brown eyes concerned. "I'm not mad," Katie murmured soothingly to the horse as soon as she could make her lungs work again. "It wasn't your fault. I know it wasn't. I never should have rushed you like that."

The horse whinnied softly as if to urge her to her feet. "I need to get up. I know. Give me a minute."

Susan stood placidly next to her, and after a moment Katie summoned the will to grab hold of a stirrup and try to pull herself up. She made it as far as her knees before blinding pain shot from her right ankle, the one she'd landed on.

She cried out and collapsed onto the snow again.

All she needed was a broken ankle. No, she thought when she realized she could still rotate it, it probably was just a sprain. It only seemed to hurt when she put weight on it.

But how was she going to mount without putting weight on her ankle? She would just have to push through the pain, she thought. The alternative was waiting here for Peter to find her.

She forced herself to her knees again. This time she didn't even make it to her feet before a vicious cramp hit her low in the abdomen. Katie gasped as hot waves radiated through her.

The baby!

In the initial shock from her fall and pain from the sprained ankle, she had completely forgotten about the tiny life inside her.

Another cramp hit her, stronger than the first, and she clutched at her abdomen and doubled over.

Oh, please, God, no! Panic flashed through her. She couldn't lose this baby. She *couldn't*.

She needed help. She needed to get out of this cold and find help right now!

Her breath came in little sobbing gasps as she cried and prayed at the same time, all the while she struggled to make it into the saddle. By sheer stubbornness, she managed to climb to her feet and stood on one foot, clinging to the pommel. Another cramp racked her.

Above her moan she heard dogs barking from behind her.

She turned and saw Luke and Millie approaching, with Peter behind them leading the pack horse.

"Oh, Peter. Help me!"

His eyes widened with shock as he took in her dishevelment and the panic she knew must be abundantly clear on her features.

He dismounted and rushed to her in one quick motion. "What happened? Are you all right?"

"Susan stumbled and I fell off. I need a doctor, Peter. It's urgent. You're going to have to leave the ranch and go for help."

He grabbed her arm. "What is it? Sit down. You shouldn't be moving around like that. You might have a spinal injury."

"I don't have a spinal injury. I need a doctor. Right now!"

Another wave of pain hit her and she clutched at her abdomen, moaning in distress. Oh, it hurt. Far, far worse than the physical pain was the guilt and self-loathing surging through her.

How could she have been foolish enough to risk her baby's life over hurt feelings and a stupid argument?

She should have been more careful.

She had no business even being up on a horse. Really, she shouldn't be here in Wyoming. If she cared about her child's safety, she would have been safe and warm in her quiet condo in Lake Oswego, not out here in the cold and snow and wind.

She sobbed again and Peter pulled her close. "You're scaring me, Katie. Tell me what's wrong. Where do you hurt? Do you think you might have internal injuries?"

She had to tell him. None of the reasons for keeping her pregnancy a secret mattered now, not when their child's life was at stake.

"I'm pregnant and I'm cramping. I don't want to lose this baby. Please, Peter. Help me!"

For several seconds Peter could only stare at her as her words seemed to echo in the cold, still air.

Pregnant? *Pregnant?*

He barely had time to register the concept before she was struggling frantically to mount her horse again.

A million questions poured through him, but he knew the most important thing now was taking care of her.

"Stop. You're going to fall again, Katie. Let me help you. Are you sure you can ride?"

"I don't have any other choice. It would take me too long to walk through the snow to the ranch house. And I don't think I could. I think I may have sprained my ankle."

He tried to figure out another way to get her back to the house but couldn't, so he carefully lifted her into the saddle. She clutched the reins as he led the way back, her face set against the pain and her breathing ragged.

The ride seemed to take forever and he couldn't concentrate on anything but seeing her safely settled. By the time they reached the ranch house, she was pale and trembling and he knew she was in pain.

"Hang on," he said in what he hoped was a reassuring tone. "We're almost there."

She didn't answer. Her eyes were huge, frightened. He rode all the way to the front porch and jumped from his horse and quickly tied the reins to a hitching post there. He reached up and pulled her from the horse and into his arms, then carried her into the house.

He carried her to the couch and lowered her gingerly. "What do you need me to do? Where can I go for help?"

"Check the phone first. Maybe service has been restored."

He lifted the receiver and the dial tone in his ear was the sweetest sound he'd ever heard. "It works. Should I call an ambulance?"

She appeared to think it over, then shook her head. "I doubt the roads out here in the rural areas have been plowed enough for one to make it through. Even with four-wheel drive, I don't know that we could make it to the clinic in Daniel."

"What can we do?"

"My friend, Laura Harp, is a doctor. She lives just a few ranches over and could probably make it to Sweetwater by snowmobile. I'll call her."

He handed the phone to Katie, who whipped off her gloves and punched in a number. While he stood by, hating his helplessness, she explained the situation to someone on the other end of the line.

"Yes, I'm sure. Thirteen weeks gestation, eleven weeks since conception," she murmured into the phone. He didn't miss the furtive look she sent in his direction.

He did a quick mental calculation back to their passionate night together before Christmas. The dates were definitely right, but he didn't need that extra proof to convince him the unbelievable truth his heart was already telling him.

The child she carried was his.

He had no doubt in his mind whatsoever. So many things made sense now. How stunned she had been to see him when he showed up at the ranch, her on-again, off-again sickness, the light-headedness, the secrets he had glimpsed several time in her eyes.

He wondered if she had had any intention at all of telling him. Somehow he didn't think so. He drew in a sharp breath at the idea that if she hadn't fallen and been forced to tell him, he might have spent his entire life never knowing he had fathered a child.

Later. He could think about all that later. Now he needed to do everything he could to help that child survive.

Katie hung up the phone. "She should be here within a half hour. Laura's a wonderful doctor. If anyone can save my baby, she can."

Though the questions crowding his mind begged to be asked, he knew this wasn't the time. "We need to get you into something dry."

"You're right," she said after a slight pause. "Would you mind helping me into my bedroom? I have a robe there I can put on."

"Of course," he answered, frustrated at her obvious reluctance to ask him for help, even in something as minor as this.

He scooped her from the couch and carried her down the hall to her bedroom. Through the tumult in his mind, he registered that her room was similar to his, decorated in mountain-lodge style with river rock and wood and natural colors.

He set her on the edge of a low trunk at the foot of the bed and knelt to pull her boots off first, then helped her out of her heavy insulated coveralls. She was wet clear through, and guilt swamped him as he remembered dumping snow on her. She was pregnant and he had just spent fifteen minutes throwing snowballs at her, for hell's sake.

"Thank you," she murmured. "If you'll just hand me that robe over the chair there, I believe I can handle it from here."

He complied then went to work building a fire in the stone fireplace. By the time the kindling caught, she had changed into her robe and started to hop from the chest to the bed.

"Damn it, Katie. Let me help."

Just as he moved to her side, she gasped again and clutched her stomach. He lifted her, struck by how fragile she felt in his arms, then tucked her into the bed.

"I'm so scared, Peter." Her voice sounded small, hollow.

"I know. I wish I could make it better."

He didn't know how to handle this powerless feeling. He wasn't used to it. In his world, he thrived on challenges but this was a force he could do nothing against. He wanted to make everything all right again, to ease her fear and her pain, and he hated that he couldn't.

She gripped his hand tightly. "I should have told you. I'm sorry."

The words surprised him and he didn't know how to respond. "We can talk about that later. Right now you just need to rest until the doctor gets here."

She nodded and even closed her eyes for a moment, her hand still gripping his. He watched her, not sure if she was sleeping.

A strange warmth started low in his chest, then pulsed through him. It took him a few moments to identify what he was feeling. When he realized it was tenderness, he wanted to drop her hand and get the hell out of there as fast as he could run. He forced himself to gently set her fingers onto the quilt instead.

She opened her eyes. "Please don't leave."

"I'm only going to see if the power has been restored along with the phone service. I'll be back, I promise."

She seemed satisfied with that and closed her eyes again.

A quick look at the power situation confirmed what he'd been hoping. They had electricity again. He shut off the generator and switched the household current back and was returning the bedroom when the doorbell rang.

The doctor. Hallelujah!

Laura Harp was at least sixty, petite and with short steel-gray hair and incongruously trendy tiny dark-rimmed glasses. She looked more like a librarian than a country doctor, until he looked into her vivid blue eyes and saw a mixture of warmth and concern and aeons of wisdom and experience he couldn't even begin to comprehend.

"That was quick."

"I've got a wicked-fast Polaris. Comes in real handy during weeks like this. It's the only way I've been able to get into the clinic since Thursday. You must be a friend of Katherine's."

He wouldn't go that far. But since he didn't know how else to characterize their relationship, he merely nodded. "Peter Logan."

Behind those glasses, her eyes widened with recognition. He could tell from her expression that she must be familiar with his name. He could only guess by her surprise that she must have heard about the infamous Logan-Crosby feud.

"Katie is lying down back here."

He led the way down the hall to the bedroom. Katie's eyelids fluttered open when he opened the door and her gaze immediately went to the small woman at his side.

"You're here," she breathed, with such palpable relief in her eyes that he felt large and male and out of place.

"I need to go take care of the horses and stable them. I'll, um, just get out of your way."

He escaped without giving either of them the chance to argue—not that he thought they would.

Outside, he filled his lungs with icy air, then let it out in a rush. At last he could come to terms with the stunning events of the last hour.

Pregnant.

If this Dr. Harp succeeded in saving the baby, he would be a father in a little over six months.

This was huge. Gigantic. So staggering, he couldn't manage to work his mind around it. How could this have happened? Despite the fire and heat of that incredible night together, they had been scrupulously careful. He had used a condom every time.

Except one, he suddenly remembered. He had awakened sometime during the night, already aroused, and had been inside her before he was really conscious of it. He thought he had pulled out in time but obviously at least one little swimmer had hit the jackpot.

A baby.

A baby with Katherine *Crosby*!

What the hell was he supposed to do now? He stood there in the cold Wyoming air, gazing at the raw, snow-covered mountains, overwhelmed by the reality that his entire life was about to change.

Another man would probably think it best all around if Katie lost the baby.

He blew out a breath that clouded in the cold. Yeah, his life might be far less complicated if she miscarried but just the possibility filled him with a hard, spiny knot under his breastbone.

Kate already loved their unborn child. He had seen it in the hand she splayed protectively over her abdomen, in the fear in her eyes, in her frantic call for help.

Losing the baby would devastate her.

Despite everything—her deception that night and, really, in the weeks since when she should have told him about the baby—he didn't want to see her hurt.

What if he hadn't been here? If he hadn't been so determined to find her after he learned who she was and hadn't flown out from Portland despite the storm warning?

His blood ran cold thinking about it.

She would have been trapped out here for days, pregnant and alone, having to take care of all the stock by herself.

The horses, still hitched to the rail out front, stamped in the snow, and the little one, Susan, whinnied impatiently, dragging him from his thoughts.

"I'm coming, I'm coming." He grabbed their reins and started walking toward the barn, struck by how surreal this all seemed. His whole world had just shifted and he wasn't quite sure how to deal with it.

Three days earlier—hell, an *hour* earlier—he knew just who he was, what he wanted out of life.

He was Peter Logan, oldest child of Leslie and Terrence, brother to Eric and David and Jillian and Bridget. He was the young CEO of the Logan Corporation and brimmed over with vibrant, ambitious plans for moving the company forward.

Now, God willing, he was going to be a father. And everything had changed.

"Isn't there something you can give me?" Katie asked after Laura had examined her. "Some pill that could stop the cramps?"

Laura squeezed her hand. "Not this early in the game, I'm afraid. I wish I had more to offer but the only thing I can prescribe at this point is plenty of rest. And don't discount the power of hope and prayers."

If hope and prayers were enough, she had more than enough of both to make all the difference. But Katie knew sometimes all the faith in the world couldn't defeat nature.

Still, she had to cling to that calm assurance in her friend's wise eyes.

"You're strong and healthy. I have high hopes you can keep the pregnancy if all goes well."

"Thank you." Katie tried to smile, but she had a feeling it was a little watery. Laura pressed a cool hand to her cheek, and the tears burning behind her eyes trickled out.

"Hey, now. What's this?" the doctor asked.

"I'm in such a mess, Laura."

"Ordinarily my policy is to mind my own business and stick to doctoring in matters like this, but we've been friends for a long time."

Despite the fear still heavy in her chest, Katie

smiled at the memory. "Ever since you gave me six stitches in my hand after my ill-fated attempt at helping Clint string some barbed wire. I must have been all of, what, seventeen?"

"Right. You've been good business. Seems like every time you come out to the ranch I get to do a little doctoring. Since we're old friends and all, I guess that gives me the right to be a little nosy and bend my strict MYOB policy. I'll just come out and ask. Does the father know you're pregnant?"

"He does now," Katie muttered. "I had no choice but to tell him after I fell."

"Ah." Somehow Laura managed to inject that single syllable with an entire world full of understanding and sympathy. "The gorgeous Mr. Logan, then?"

Katie nodded, then bit her lip when it threatened to tremble. She swallowed her tears again and blew out a breath.

"It's a long story, Laura. One I'm afraid won't have a very happy ending. I haven't been precisely truthful with him from the beginning. I misled him and…I didn't tell him about the baby. I doubt he'll ever be able to see past that."

Laura sat on the edge of the bed. "You might have made mistakes. You both might have, for all I know. But now is the time for both of you to put those differences behind you and concentrate on what's best for this baby of yours."

"I didn't want him to know."

"Here's your first parenting lesson. What you want or need doesn't really matter much anymore in the scheme of things. Your first and only priority is that baby. Whatever the circumstances, the two of you created a life together. It's up to you to do right by that little life."

"I'm going to be a terrible mother." The tears spilled free once more and trickled down her cheeks. "How can I be anything else? Just look at the kind of example I had!"

Laura handed her a tissue, then gathered her into her arms. "You'll be a wonderful mother. You have so much love inside you to give. You just have to trust yourself."

"I've already made so many mistakes."

"There's not a mother on earth who hasn't. It's a wonder I can even let my two boys out in public with all the mistakes I made. They're grown now and I'm still making mistakes with them. But you know, for all my shortcomings, they've turned out to be pretty decent people. So have you, despite your parents. You just need to trust yourself. You've always been much stronger than you've ever given yourself credit for."

Right now she felt like a weak and trembling child, especially whenever she thought about the inevitable confrontation with Peter.

"Thank you," Katie murmured.

"Rest now. Stay off that sprain until you can put weight on it without pain. I'll call tomorrow to see how you're doing, but if you need me before then, I can be here in a heartbeat. You have your young man give me a call, all right?"

Katie nodded, though she wanted to protest that Peter was *not* her young man.

When it came right down to it, that was the entire problem.

Nine

She awoke just after midnight.

With an anguished cry of alarm, she sat up and her hand automatically fluttered to her abdomen.

Peter jumped up from his chair by the fire, his heart pounding. "What is it? Another cramp?"

She frowned, as if not quite sure. After a moment she let out a breath and sagged against the pillows again. "No. I must have been dreaming."

"Not a good one, I'm guessing."

"No. It was horrible and so real. One of those dreams you try so hard to wake from."

He sat on the edge of the wide bed. "Want to tell me about it?"

Her fingers clutched the scalloped edge of the quilt she had pushed off in her sleep. "You'll think I'm crazy."

"Try me."

She closed her eyes. "I was riding Susan through thick trees and she stumbled. I fell off, just like today, but when I caught my breath, I found myself staring into the yellow eyes of a wolf. It was beautiful but terrifying at the same time. Silver with black fur around his face."

Her eyes opened and the remembered fear in them clutched his heart. "I can still see it when I close my eyes," she continued, "pacing back and forth. Pacing, endlessly pacing, until I thought I would scream."

She shuddered and pulled the blanket up to her shoulders. "Suddenly I had a baby in my arms. I'm not sure how it got there, but then the wolf started edging closer, so close I could feel the heat emanating from his fur and smell his breath. I knew, somehow I knew, he would try to wrench the baby away from me. Right before he lunged at me, I threw a snowball at him and he disappeared."

She grimaced. "Weird, isn't it? I knew you'd think I was crazy."

"I don't think you're crazy. You've had a rough day."

She looked around the room, at the dark windows. "What time is it?"

"Around midnight. How are you feeling?"

She touched her abdomen again, as if for reassurance. He wondered if she knew she slept that way, with one hand tucked under her cheek and the other curled around the tiny life growing inside her. All evening long he had watched her sleep as he tried to come to terms with the shock of finding out he was going to become a father.

"I'm fine. My ankle throbs but the rest of me seems okay."

"You slept through dinner. Are you hungry?"

Her brow furrowed as if she had to think about it. "I guess I am, a little," she said after a moment. "But you don't have to wait on me. I can find something."

"Don't even think about it," he said sternly. "I talked to Dr. Harp before she took off and she said she wants you on bed rest for at least the next few days. I'll fix you something."

"I don't want you to have to do that."

"Is there anyone else lurking around Sweetwater I don't know about who can feed you?"

"You know there's not."

"Right. A smart woman like you should know when she's all out of choices."

"Whoever said I was smart?" she muttered, looking so disgruntled he almost laughed.

He knew damn well she was brilliant. She had told him she'd been admitted to Stanford early and he knew she had graduated with honors.

He also knew enough about the inner workings at Crosby to know her brother Trent relied heavily on her brains and that she had revitalized research and development at the company under her tenure.

Brains and beauty. His baby could do a whole lot worse in a mother, he thought.

"Just give me a minute," he said.

When he returned fifteen minutes later with a tray, she was reading a pregnancy book with a photograph of a smiling baby on the cover. She set it down, coloring a little, he was charmed to see.

"I'm overwhelmed by all the things I never knew about pregnancy and childbirth. It's terrifying."

"Not nearly as frightening as what comes after the delivery," he pointed out.

"Don't think that hasn't been giving me nightmares, too."

She paused and her fingers clutched the edge of the quilt again, her expression a jumbled mix of emotions, determination in the forefront.

"Peter, I—"

"Omelettes taste like rubber school erasers when they're cold. For the baby's sake and for your own, you need to eat," he said, cutting her off. He knew what was coming. Yes, they would talk about her pregnancy and all the ramifications of it. They *had* to talk about it.

But he wasn't ready yet.

Though she looked as if she wanted to argue, he gave her his best don't-mess-with-me look and she finally turned that determination to the tray he set in front of her.

"This is delicious!" she exclaimed after a moment.

"You sound surprised."

"I don't know. I suppose I wouldn't have expected the Logan CEO to be a culinary whiz."

He laughed. "I'm far from that. Mom insisted each of us have at least one specialty in the kitchen. Since I've always been an early riser, I was relegated to breakfast food by default. Besides omelettes, I also make a wicked French toast."

He suddenly had the sobering realization that he knew relatively little about this woman who was pregnant with his child. "What about you? Do you like to cook?"

She took a sip of the juice he had included on the tray, then set the glass down at the same time she shrugged. "Too much. I also like to eat. That's why I used to be huge."

"I don't remember you as huge."

She studied him for several moments, her expression unreadable. "You don't remember me at all, do you?"

Again he tried to conjure up an image of her from before that night at the charity auction. He *should* remember her. Damn it, why couldn't he? "You used to have glasses and long, pretty hair, right?"

"And an extra forty pounds."

"I don't remember that part."

She rolled her eyes and laughed. "As if you would admit it, even if you did remember."

"We Logan men have never been dumb."

He paused and his smile slid away. "Although I certainly was three months ago. I should have recognized you. I'm sorry."

"Don't apologize. My own family barely knew me when I walked into the benefit. I've been hiding for a long time behind the image people expected to see when they looked at me."

What did people expect to see when they looked at her? he wondered. And what was she hiding from? He wanted to ask but he sensed she already regretted her comment.

"Why didn't you tell me who you were?" he asked instead.

He had posed the same question to her before, after he first arrived at Sweetwater, but she had brushed him off with some glib answer about being carried away by the glamour and excitement of pretending to be someone else for a while.

He hadn't bought it then. Now he didn't know what to believe.

She set her fork down next to her half-eaten omelette and let out a slow breath.

"I suppose I was shocked and flattered when you seemed interested," she admitted. "I've always been in the shadows, one of those women no one noticed. I didn't mind. I preferred it that way. But suddenly one of Portland's most eligible bachelors was flirting with me—*me,* fat, awkward Katie Crosby—and I didn't want it to end. I knew the moment you learned I was a Crosby you wouldn't be able to get away from me fast enough so I—I lied."

There was more to this story, he thought. Why had she gone home with him? He had learned enough about her since he arrived at the ranch that he had a feeling her actions that night had been as uncharacteristic for her as they'd been for him.

It had been far easier to accuse her of corporate thievery than to dig into his own psyche and ask himself why he had responded to her so instantly and so passionately—and why she had reacted to him the same way.

"And the baby?" he asked. "Were you ever going to tell me you were pregnant?"

He hadn't meant to ask the question, but somehow the words forced their way out.

She met his gaze for just a moment, her expression guarded, then gazed at the fire. "No," she finally said.

He was completely unprepared for the pain that pierced through him at her answer. "Why not?"

Her laugh was short, harsh. "A million reasons. You didn't even know my real name. I'm sorry but I couldn't quite figure out a good way to suddenly show up at your doorstep and say, 'Hey, remember me? Funny thing, my name isn't really Celeste, it's Katherine Crosby. Yes, of *those* Crosbys, the family you hate. Nice to meet you. Oh, and by the way, guess what? Great news! We're having a baby.'"

Without a pause Peter asked, "Didn't you think I had a right to know?"

Her gaze shifted to the fire. "I couldn't think about that, not with everything between us. I don't know, maybe I would have told you eventually, but to be honest, all I've been able to focus on for the last week has been my own shock. I haven't even had time to get used to the idea myself."

And yet he knew she already loved the child they had created together.

"So where do we go from here?" he asked.

"A baby was something neither of us ever expected. I don't know how or why it happened, not when we were so careful, but I do know I want this child, Peter. I don't expect anything from you. Tomorrow the roads should be clear enough for travel. You can go back to Portland and forget any of this ever happened."

A muscle clenched in his jaw. "You think I would just walk away from you and the baby? You must think I'm a real son of a bitch."

"I don't think that of you at all! I just don't want you to feel obligated to stick around and pretend to be happy about all of this. I know it's been a shock."

He wanted to laugh at the understatement but he could find very little humor in this whole thing.

He had thought of nothing but the future while he had sat by the fire watching her sleep. In that darkened room, he had gone over the very limited options

available to them now that they had a child to consider and had come up with only one real solution.

"We should get married."

At his blunt words, her gaze flew to his and her
mouth sagged open. She swallowed hard several times
then shook her head vigorously. If she could have gotten out of bed, he had no doubt she would have stalked
out of the room. "No. Absolutely not. Forget it!"

"Just like that? You're not even going to think
about it?"

"What's to think about? As far as proposals go—
if that's what you want to call that…proclamation—
this one is both unnecessary and unwanted."

"I disagree."

He didn't see any other choice available to them.
Wherever possible, a child needed both parents. He
believed it fiercely. His parents would expect them
to marry when they learned a child was involved.

He expected it.

Getting married was the right thing to do, and
since that day the Logans had plucked him out of a
bleak future and given him the world, he had spent
his life always trying to do the right thing.

Katherine held her ground. "No. I am perfectly capable of raising my child by myself. I don't need you."

"Not *your* child," he said coolly. "*Our* child."

"You're the sperm donor. That's all."

He narrowed his gaze and refused to let her see
how those words wounded him. "Is that why you se-

duced me that night? The old biological clock was ticking away and you decided you needed a warm, healthy male? What did you do, poke a few holes in one of the condoms and think I'd never find out?"

Even if he had believed his own words, the shock on her features would have told him how ludicrous that idea was.

"Of course not!" she exclaimed. "I *never* expected to end up pregnant from that night. This was as much a shock to me as it is to you! I didn't believe it myself. I denied it as long as possible until I could no longer avoid facing the truth. I never would have tricked you like that."

"And I'm supposed to believe you, *Celeste?*"

She flushed but met his gaze steadily. "All the more reason why your marriage offer is completely ridiculous. You don't like me or trust me. How are we supposed to base a marriage on that?"

"We'll just have to figure it out as we go along."

"We won't have to figure *anything* out because I'm not going to marry you!"

"This is my child, too. I intend to be part of his life."

"Or her life."

"Either way. I've got no preference."

"Fine. You can be involved. You don't have to marry me to do that. People find themselves in this situation all the time. They manage to work it out."

"To the satisfaction of no one involved," he pointed out, "especially not the child."

"You think a marriage between two people who barely know each other is the answer?"

"So we'll get to know each other. And then we'll get married."

Katie wanted to scream at his resolute tone. Of all the scenarios she had imagined for this conversation, this was a direction she absolutely never expected him to take. Marriage! Between a Crosby and a Logan. The idea was laughable.

This was no Romeo and Juliet. She wouldn't marry him. She *couldn't*. It would be disastrous all the way around. Her feelings for him were already too complicated, too intense. She wouldn't be able to bear trapping him in a loveless marriage.

She had seen the hell of her parents' marriage. The fierce fights, the cheating on both sides. They had stayed together far too long, not for the sake of the children—that novel idea never would have occurred to them—but because neither Jack nor Sheila wanted to be the one to cry uncle.

They must have loved each other at some point. She had to believe that. But by the time they divorced, that love had morphed into something ugly and bitter.

A marriage without even that foundation at the beginning didn't stand a chance—and an innocent child would be the one to suffer.

"No," she said almost frantically. "No. I won't do it."

Something of her distress must have shown on her features, in her tone, because Peter crossed the room, his expression concerned and faintly guilty. "Don't upset yourself about this right now. I'm sorry, I shouldn't have pushed you. You need to rest and take it easy, not argue with me. We have time to sort everything out."

Maybe they wouldn't have anything to sort out. The fear she had been holding at bay seeped through as she remembered just what challenges their child faced before entering the world. Maybe the pregnancy wouldn't survive and all this talk about marriage would be moot.

No. She wouldn't think like that. *You've always been much stronger than you've ever given yourself credit for,* Laura had said. She had to believe she could be strong for her baby—for *their* baby.

"Thank you for the omelette," she said to Peter. "Your mother would be proud."

"Of my cooking skills anyway," he said, just a shadow of bitterness in his voice. "I'll leave you to rest now. I'll be out on the couch. Call me if you need anything."

She nodded, then watched him carry the tray out of the room, wondering how it was that telling him about their child had left her feeling more alone than ever.

"No spotting at all and no cramping since yesterday afternoon, then?"

"Nothing," Katie answered Laura the next day when she stopped at the ranch before heading to the clinic. "I'm a little queasy but other than that, I feel great."

She had been too nauseated to even finish the French toast Peter prepared for her, though the few mouthfuls she'd been able to swallow had indeed tasted delicious, crispy and sweet and covered in cinnamon sugar.

"Most pregnant mothers have a hard time accepting it, but believe it or not, queasy can be a good sign," the doctor said. "Still, I'd like to hook up the Doppler here and listen to the baby's heartbeat."

"Can you do that this early?" Peter asked from where he stood by the window. The day before he had escaped to the barn while Laura was here but today he seemed reluctant to leave during her exam.

"We should be able to find it. You're thirteen weeks along, right?"

Katie nodded.

"Let's see what we've got, then."

Upon the doctor's instructions, Katie bared her midriff, chagrined at herself for feeling exposed with Peter in the room. The man had seen far more of her than her belly, she reminded herself. Still, that had been under far different circumstances. She couldn't help being a little uncomfortable in this intimate situation.

She forgot about her unease when Laura rubbed a small device over her abdomen. Immediately a loud pulsing filled the room.

"That's your heartbeat there," the doctor said, then passed the sensor across her skin again, pressing a little harder this time. After a moment the beats accelerated noticeably and Laura smiled widely. "And that's your baby's. You can tell because it's much faster than yours. It's a beautiful sound, isn't it?"

To Katie's deep embarrassment, tears began to glide down her cheeks. "Wonderful."

She was stunned when Peter crossed the room and sat beside her on the bed with an odd, stunned expression on his face. He placed his hand over hers and squeezed her fingers.

"Is the baby all right?" he asked Laura.

"I can't really tell without an ultrasound, but the heartbeat is strong and healthy, just the way I like them. You're not out of the woods yet, Katie my girl, but if you can make it to the second trimester—generally considered to be around fourteen weeks—the chance of miscarriage drops quite a bit. That's only another week for you."

"Is it safe for her to travel? Can I fly her home to Portland?"

Laura looked pensively at Katie. "That's a tricky one. Ordinarily I'd recommend at least a few days bed rest to give your body time to heal. That was a nasty fall and even if you weren't pregnant, I'd suggest taking it easy for a while. With that bum ankle, you could fall again, which wouldn't be good for you or the baby."

She put her equipment away in her bag. "When you're so close to the magic number of fourteen weeks, I guess I would err on the side of caution and suggest you lay low until then." She shrugged. "On the other hand, if it came down to a choice between staying out here by yourself or flying back to Portland, I'd have to go with Door Number Two."

Peter spoke up. "She's not by herself. I'll stay with her."

Katie swiped her eyes with the tissue the doctor handed her and stared at Peter, certain she must have misheard. "You can't take an entire week away from Logan to baby-sit me!"

"Why not?"

"Because you're—you're the CEO. Don't you have work? Mergers, meetings, that kind of thing?"

"I'm surrounded by excellent people. They can run things for a while without me, I'm sure. Don't worry, Crosby. The company won't fall apart in a week."

She couldn't believe he would consent to stay. He had already been stuck here for four days and she knew how restless he was to return to work. She wanted to tell him to go, to assure him she would be fine for a few days, even though she was so tempted to lean against him for a while.

"I can't ask you to do that," she said finally.

"You didn't. I'm offering. No, not offering, insisting."

Laura stood. "I'm going to wisely stay out of this

and head over to the Bar S to check on Darwin's broken leg. Let me know how it all shakes out, though my money's on Mr. Logan here."

Katie thanked her friend for coming out to the ranch and bid her goodbye. She waited until Laura left before she turned on Peter. "You can't possibly stay another week."

"You would rather take on the world and come out swinging than admit when you're backed against a wall, wouldn't you? I'm staying, Katie. Deal with it. Anyway, with the phones back up, I can find plenty of work to do from here. Don't worry about me."

She didn't worry about him, she admitted. She worried about herself. Her emotions were already so vulnerable. She wanted desperately to lean on him for a while and she hated herself for it.

She was a strong, capable woman who could handle pregnancy on her own. But as he had said the night before, she was also smart enough to know when she was all out of choices.

Ten

For a woman who had never been wooed before, re-sisting Peter Logan was proving an impossible task.

Like her brother Trent, Peter was a man used to getting what he wanted. Right now he seemed to want her—or at least the baby she carried. With the same single-minded purpose and determination that made him a formidable business opponent, the blasted man was doing everything he could to attain his goal.

He was charming, he was sweet, he was attentive. He brought her meals in bed and played games and watched old movies with her. Without a single mur-mur of complaint, he cared for the animals and made sure they had a steady supply of firewood.

He told her stories about growing up with the Logans—about family vacations and campouts in the backyard and playing basketball in the driveway.

Even more seductive, he listened to her. Genuinely listened.

As if a cork had been yanked from her mouth, she found herself telling him far more than she intended.

She told him about how shy and awkward she'd been as a girl, how Trent had basically raised her because Sheila had been too busy with her social life and Jack had been too busy with his business. She told him about her fascination with computers and how she had turned to books out of her loneliness at boarding school.

She even found herself telling him about Steve. Not the whole ugly story, but enough that he knew she had been bitterly hurt and betrayed and had broken off her engagement.

He was the perfect listener, he didn't comment in all the wrong places or try to give unwanted advice. He simply made her feel as if nothing else mattered to him at that moment in time except the words spilling out of her mouth.

The right-brain, intellectual side recognized his attention as a carefully calculated, even cynical, attempt to sway her to his way of thinking. For some ridiculous reason, he seemed to think they needed to get married for their baby's sake and he was doing everything he could to convince her they could make it work.

The left-brain, emotional side had to confess it was working.

Three days after she fell off her horse, nearly a week after both he and the storm blew into Sweetwater, Katie sat curled up on the couch in the great room with a book on her lap while Peter worked on a report on his laptop computer.

As she listened to the click of keys under his strong, elegant hands and watched the fire flicker over those masculine features, she wondered how she could ever return to life without him.

She loved him.

Because he had come to her rescue so many years ago, she had always considered him a kind man. But during these last few days of nearly constant togetherness, she had come to see him as a decent and honorable one, a man who tried fiercely to please his family and who treated his responsibilities with solemn care.

How pathetic was that? Chubby, shy Katie Crosby, in love with the gorgeous and dynamic Peter Logan. Wouldn't her mother just about screech the house down if she ever found out? And not just because he was a Logan, either, although Sheila would certainly have a fit about that.

How could you ever think you had a chance with a man like him? She could almost hear her mother's derision echoing in her head. *You would have to be out of your mind to think Peter Logan would even look twice at you.*

And yet he seemed serious about them marrying. He hadn't let a day go by without renewing his proposal. She hated herself but she could feel her resolve weaken, despite her best efforts to shore it up.

The idea of sharing a future with him was just so tantalizing. These three days alone with him here had been wonderful, the best of her life. She caught herself a dozen times trying to store a memory in her mind. The smell of him just after a shower: soap and aftershave and sexy maleness. The feel of his strong fingers tucking a fleece blanket over her knees. The sight of him through the window as he threw a stick into the snow for Luke and Millie to chase.

She couldn't bear knowing she would have very few more of those memories. But this wasn't real life. They were suspended in a cheerful little bubble here, away from her family and his, away from the pressures of life in Portland. She couldn't pretend that just because they'd been able to live together well here at Sweetwater they could enjoy a happy marriage.

How could they, when he would be marrying her only out of that damn sense of responsibility he took so seriously? He didn't love her. A marriage in which only one person loved the other would be a nightmare of unimaginable pain.

No, she had to be strong and withstand his insidious assault on her willpower. The happily-ever-after she might secretly long for would never happen. She needed to accept that and prepare her heart for its inevitable fracture.

"What put that grim look on your face all of a sudden?" he asked. "Are you having a pain?"

She blinked away her depressing thoughts to find him watching her with concern in his dark eyes. "No. The baby is fine. I haven't had any pains since the day I fell."

"The ankle bugging you?"

"No. It's almost back to normal. I barely even notice when I put weight on it now."

"Then what is it?"

For a moment she debated how to answer him. When she couldn't come up with a plausible lie, she plunged ahead with the truth. "I've enjoyed these few days. I'm going to be sorry to see them end."

Oh, she shouldn't have admitted that, she thought when Peter raised an eyebrow, as if her confession surprised him as much as it did her.

"It doesn't have to end," he said. "Not if you marry me."

She shook her head in exasperation, though she could feel her heart splinter a little more around the edges. "I can't figure out if you're relentless or simply ruthless."

He grinned. "I'm both. You've played poker with me. Haven't you figured that out? You owe me something like eight hundred matchsticks by now, don't you?"

"Only because you cheat!"

"I prefer to think I'm innovative and think outside the box."

She laughed and tossed a pillow at him, grateful for the diversion from her melancholy. "I prefer to think you're a dirty rotten cheat who makes up his own rules."

"You're just sore because you never knew a pair of sixes automatically trumps every other possible hand. I'm telling you, it's the Holy Grail of five-card stud. Ask anyone."

"I can't believe you tried to pull that one. Or that you thought I was stupid enough to fall for it."

"Hey, a guy's got to try."

When he looked at her with that smile in his eyes, she almost thought maybe they could make a marriage work.

"How's the work going?" she asked.

"Surprisingly well. I'd forgotten what a little change in scenery can do for the creative juices. I've been able to accomplish more in just a couple hours a day here than I do putting in eighty-hour work weeks."

Despite his protestations that the company could run fine in his absence, she had to wonder what the other top brass at Logan thought about their CEO taking off to the wilds of Wyoming for a week.

She hadn't dared to ask him—or to ask if his family knew what he was doing here.

He hadn't been exactly inaccessible. Since the phones had been restored, she knew he e-mailed his staff regularly and had at least one lengthy phone conversation with his assistant each day. That interaction was minimal compared to what she knew her father would have been doing in the same situation.

Jack would have been a basket case. She remembered once he and Sheila had come to Switzerland for a parents' weekend at her boarding school—the only such event she could ever remember them attending—and her father had barely taken the phone away from his ear long enough to eat.

Peter was not her father. If she had learned anything these last few days it was that clear fact. She knew his work was important to him but it didn't seem to consume him.

He didn't seem to mind the interruption. After closing his laptop, he joined her on the couch and reached for her hand. That was another thing she had learned about Peter Logan during this time alone with him. He was more physically affectionate than she ever would have expected. He seemed to enjoy touching her, caressing her fingers, rubbing her shoulders, even kissing her casually on the cheek.

She wasn't used to it and didn't know quite how to respond but she had to admit she found it both sweet and disarming.

"Speaking of innovation and outside-the-box

ideas," he said, holding firm to her fingers, "I've been thinking about something."

She eyed him warily. "What?"

"Our families have wasted years and untold resources competing with each other. How much more successful would we both be if we could channel some of that negative energy into cooperating on certain projects?"

She stared at him, unable to believe the words were actually coming from him. The Crosbys and the Logans working together without the business world jerking to a complete standstill? Was it even possible?

"What kind of projects?" she asked.

"This super-router, for example. With your NPIC software system and the NPIR hardware we're developing, between Crosby and Logan we could create the fastest networking system the world has ever known. Both those components could of course be purchased separately but how much more effective would they be if we packaged them together? Made them one-hundred-percent compatible?"

"The industry wouldn't know what hit it." Her mind raced, imagining the possibilities. Trent had long talked about coming up with their own super-router hardware to complement the software they had put much of their design efforts into, but any project they started would be years behind Logan in development.

"You're not talking about a merger, right?"

"No. Just a cooperative agreement on this project. And maybe if it was successful, we could look into working together on other projects down the line."

"It has potential," she admitted.

"I think it's brilliant."

She smiled at his arrogance, then sobered when she thought of all the ramifications to be considered, especially the single overriding concern. "Our families would never agree to work together. Not with all that's gone on between us."

"They might be more willing if we can find a way to bridge the gap between the Logans and the Crosbys. What better way to do that than if we married and gave them all a shared grandchild?" His thumb caressed her knuckle. "Marry me, Katie."

She stared at him, tempted beyond words. Oh, how she wanted to say yes. She closed her eyes, trying to draw courage from somewhere deep inside her to turn him down, even though she desperately wanted to agree.

"Peter, I—"

She didn't know exactly how she would have answered him. Whatever words hovered on her tongue were interrupted by the phone ringing.

They stared at each other for a moment, then with a sigh Peter reached for it, as nearly all the calls in the last three days had been for him.

"Hello?"

After a moment his features froze into an expression of acute dislike. "Yes. She's here. One moment, please."

He handed the cordless phone to Katie. She frowned, not sure what had put that icy look on his face, that chill in his voice.

With some degree of trepidation, she took it from him. The moment she said hello, she understood. Her stomach dropped to her toes as her mother's smoky voice filled her ear.

"You have a man there? Why, Katie, you sly thing. Who is it? One of those boring computer nerds from work?"

With Sheila's animosity toward all things Logan, she certainly couldn't tell her mother Peter Logan was sitting on the couch with her. "No one," she murmured. "Um, just a friend."

"What friend? Anyone I know?"

"No, I don't believe so."

She had enough experience dealing with her mother to know she had to quickly deflect Sheila's attention to something else.

"Where are you? I thought you were staying in Tuscany until the end of the month."

To her relief, Sheila allowed herself to be sidetracked. "That was the plan but I was bored out of my mind after two days. The place was *horrible!* Absolutely ghastly. All anyone wanted to talk about was their food and their wine and how beautiful the countryside was."

Which meant that no one wanted to focus on Sheila's favorite topic—herself.

"If you ask me, one vineyard looks the same as the next. I mean, what's the big deal? It's a pile of dirt and straggly twigs. Clue in!"

Though she wanted to hang up, she knew the part she was expected to play to appease Sheila's narcissism.

"Did your friend return early with you?" Katie asked.

"Who? Gianni? He was as disappointing as Tuscany. I must tell you, he sadly misrepresented himself as some kind of rich Italian stallion. I guess one out of three wasn't bad; at least he was Italian. He just wanted to sponge off my money. I couldn't *wait* to get out of there. I left him in Milan and caught the first flight back."

Sheila paused only long enough to take a breath. "Speaking of hellholes, I don't know what you're doing in that primitive armpit but I need you to get back to Portland right now. You'll laugh about this, I'm sure, but there's the most ludicrous rumor going around that you were seen kissing *Peter Logan* at some event or other around Christmas."

She closed her eyes at the sheer loathing in her mother's voice when she said Peter's name. Here it comes, she thought. The confrontation she had been expecting. "Oh?"

"Yes! That brainless society reporter for the

Weekly even ran a picture he claims is the two of you together in some steamy kiss. Can you believe that? I haven't seen the picture yet but Penelope Danner phoned me in Italy and told me all about it. You need to do damage control right away and have those idiots run a correction. As if you'd even be caught dead anywhere near that bastard!"

Katie's gaze fell on Peter, who had absently pulled her feet into his lap and was rubbing her toes through her thick socks. "Um, right."

"Besides, Peter Logan can have his pick of any woman in Portland. Why would he bother with you?"

Ah. She should have been expecting that one, too, but it still managed to slice at her self-confidence with brutal efficacy. "That's a very good question," she said quietly.

Sheila went on as if she hadn't heard her, which was probably true. "When will you be going back to Portland?"

"I'm not sure right now. Most likely by the end of the week." *And then wouldn't the you-know-what hit the fan?*

"Good. I need you to talk to your brother."

"Which one?"

"Who do you think? As if Danny has anything to do with anybody out in that isolation chamber of his. No, I'm talking about Trent, Mr. Holier-than-Thou, unnatural child. Ever since your father named him CEO, he thinks he can run the world. You're just about the only one he listens to. Maybe you can talk some sense into him. But you need to do it in person, not from that godforsaken ranch."

She sighed. "What did he do?"

"Nothing yet, but he'd like to. If Trent had his way, I'd be stuck in some retirement condo in Arizona wearing muumuus and watching game shows all day. He doesn't want me to have any fun. Now he's threatening to use his influence to have my country club membership yanked. Can you believe that?"

"What did you do to provoke him?"

"How do you know I did anything?" Sheila asked, affront in her voice.

Because I know you, she thought. *Because I have spent twenty-eight years being one of the many victims of your lies and manipulations and petty jealousies.*

She didn't say that, of course. "Trent rarely does anything without a good reason."

"I should have known you would take his side."

Of course, Katie wanted to say. *Why wouldn't I, when Trent has been more of a parent to me than either you or Jack combined?*

"I'm not taking any sides," she murmured. "I just wanted to know why Trent is angry with you."

"Because he's a tight-assed spoilsport, that's why. He's all bent out of shape because I found out some good dirt on the Logans' precious baby factory."

"Children's Connection?"

She regretted her instinctive question when Peter

paused the foot rub, his interest sharpened. Oh, she was glad he couldn't hear Sheila's end of the conversation, especially with the venom in her mother's tone.

"It's pathetic the way the Logans throw money at that place, especially since it's nothing but a big joke. It's scandalous, that's what it is. A big fat scam. If Portland knew all the chaos surrounding that place, they would be outraged. First that Sanders baby was kidnapped and now there are rumors about a black-market baby ring operating out of the place. I even found out—I won't tell you how—that they can't even keep track of whose sperm they're giving whom."

A terrible sense of dread washed over her and she tried to avoid Peter's interested gaze. "What did you do?"

"I didn't have a chance to do anything before your brother blackmailed me to keep my mouth shut."

"What would you have done?" she asked impatiently.

"Nothing much. Just make a few phone calls to some friends in the media. Not those idiots at the *Weekly,* of course, who can't even get a photo caption right, but some of my other contacts. I would have loved to see the egg on that bitch Leslie Logan's face once the scandal broke, sending her precious clinic headed for the toilet. Can't you just see it?"

Katie closed her eyes. Nothing Sheila did should surprise her but this was vindictive, even for her.

"But you didn't say anything." She prayed that was the case.

"No. Trent told me if so much as a whiff of rumor surfaced about the stupid clinic, he would make sure I never was invited to another society event. How did I raise such an ungrateful son?"

Again, a sharp rejoinder swelled in her throat. She wished she had the courage to let it out. *You didn't raise him,* she wanted to snap. *You made Trent raise himself and then he turned around and raised the rest of us while Jack was working and you were sleeping with half of Portland.*

As usual, she bit her tongue and Sheila went on without noticing her silence. "So now you understand why you need to get back to Portland ASAP so you can handle Trent for me."

"This is between you and Trent. I'm staying out of it. And I'm not sure when I'll return to Portland. Maybe never."

The idea held enormous appeal, she had to admit. Maybe she could hide away here forever to avoid the impending storm when her mother found out about the baby.

"What's gotten into you, Katherine Celeste?" Sheila asked.

"Fresh air does wonders for a person's sanity. Maybe you ought to try it some time," she couldn't resist adding.

Peter, shamelessly eavesdropping at the end of

the couch, made a strangled noise that sounded suspiciously like a laugh. It wasn't very loud but Sheila still heard it.

"Who's there with you? Is Jack there with that slut Toni Wells?"

Sheila despised her ex-husband's second wife, the trophy wife she had always dreaded would replace her.

"Of course not!" she replied.

"Then who is it?"

"A friend," she repeated.

"Why won't you tell me who it is?"

Katie let out a frustrated breath. "Look, I have to go."

"Don't hang up! You have to talk to Trent." Her voice took on a petulant note, like a spoiled child deprived of a favorite toy.

"No," Katie said firmly. "I won't let you put me in the middle. If you want him to change his mind, you talk to him. I'm sorry, Mother. I have to go."

"Why?"

She scrambled to come up with a believable excuse. "The, um, horses need to be fed." Out of old habit, she crossed her fingers at the lie, then flushed when she caught Peter's amused look.

"Doesn't your father have people to do that?"

Katie jerked her gaze away from that smile. "Y-yes, but they're not here right now so I need to feed the stock."

She could almost hear Sheila's shudder over the phone line, but before her mother could voice her disgust of anything associated with the ranch, Katie cut her off with a hurried farewell and quickly severed the connection.

She forced herself to take several deep, carefully measured breaths to settle her nerves, just as her therapist taught her. If she needed a reminder why she and Peter could never have a happily-ever-after, Sheila had just handed her a dandy.

She couldn't marry him. Any sweet, spun-sugar fantasies she might have been silly enough to entertain, even subconsciously, dissolved into nothing under the hard rain of reality.

If she succumbed to Peter's dogged pursuit, she would be dooming them both to a future of tension and stress. Sheila despised the Logans so fiercely, Katie couldn't even imagine how she could ever tell her mother she was marrying one.

If she did, she knew Sheila's hatred would fester and eventually bubble over, coating their lives with ugliness.

It wasn't fair, she wanted to cry. Why did an old bitterness have to ruin any chance she might have of finding happiness with the man she loved?

"Is she angry?" Peter asked.

Katie shoved down the regrets and met his gaze. "Not at me. Trent is the one in her sights this time."

"That surprises me."

"Why? She and Trent are always banging heads."

"I would have expected her to blow a gasket over that photograph."

She had completely forgotten! "Oh, that. She's been in Europe and hasn't seen it yet. She's heard rumors but of course thinks everyone must be grossly mistaken."

"Why?" he asked.

If she didn't know better, she would almost have thought the puzzled look on his face was genuine. Could he really not see what was so obvious to her and to the rest of the world? Or did he just choose not to acknowledge it?

"We both know I'm not exactly the kind of woman you usually date. Portland's most gorgeous eligible bachelor and the Crosbys' fat, nerdy, ugly duckling of a daughter belong together about as much as champagne and corn dogs."

Eleven

Peter heard her words and the passion in them but didn't believe she could say them, at least with a straight face.

Ugly duckling? *Her?*

Didn't she ever look in the mirror and see the delicate features staring back at her? Those warm, expressive eyes, the elegant cheekbones, that sweetly bowed mouth that begged to be kissed?

He had been bowled over by her since that night at the charity gala, when she'd walked into the room, all grace and sophistication. From the first time she aimed that smile at him, he had been completely ensnared.

After the incredible passion they had shared, he

hadn't wanted to look at another woman. He was completely obsessed with only one. His Celeste.

Not Celeste, he corrected himself. Celeste had been a glamorous, shimmery mirage. Katie was flesh and blood, funny and stubborn and smart and real.

Even when he thought she had lied to him and deceived him, when he was sure she only slept with him to steal Logan secrets, he still hungered for her like a dying man who wants only one more moment of sunshine.

The last three days he had barely been able to take his eyes off her. She was so beautiful he couldn't look away. Knowing she was pregnant with his child filled him with awe, with wonder, with a terrifying tenderness.

He loved her.

The realization slammed into his gut like a prizefighter's uppercut. If he had been standing, he would have sagged against the ropes.

He loved Katherine Celeste Crosby.

All this time he had been trying to convince her they should marry for their child's sake. But he had only been using that as an excuse to bind her to him, he admitted now.

This couldn't be happening. He had his life carefully mapped out and he didn't have room for love in that plan—certainly not with Katie. What a mess. What a grade A, bona fide disaster.

"Peter? Are you all right?"

Katie looked concerned and even a little frightened, and he had no idea how long he had been standing there staring at her. He forced himself to smile with what he sincerely hoped was a casualness that belied his suddenly racing pulse.

"Everything's fine," he lied. "Just fine. I guess I'd better go check on the horses."

She frowned. "Because of what I said to my mother? I was just using that as an excuse to hang up the phone."

"I know you were but it's a good idea. I should still see how they're doing."

She looked unconvinced, probably because he had only come in from feeding them an hour before and they generally needed tending only once a day. He didn't care. He needed to get away *now*.

Without offering any other explanations he turned on his heel and hurried to the mudroom off the kitchen for the coveralls he used.

His thoughts a wild tangle, he fumbled to put them on and then his boots before he headed out into a frigid Wyoming afternoon.

The sky was a brilliant, cornea-scorching blue. He stood for a moment gazing at the mountains, wondering just what the hell he was supposed to do now.

If someone would have told him a week ago that he would be in love with a Crosby, he probably would have knocked their teeth out, but here he was. Somehow in the last few days her last name had ceased to matter to him. He still disliked some members of her family—her mother came immediately to mind—but he saw Katie as so much more than her name now. She was bright and funny and insightful.

The day before, she had offered a suggestion to a work dilemma he had been trying to solve long-distance and her answer had been right on the money.

These last few days had been a rare and peaceful interlude for him. He was always so busy with goals and objectives, with following the course he had charted for his life. He couldn't remember the last time he had taken time to sit and just *be*.

Being with Katie was balm to his soul. She calmed him and settled him and somehow quieted the strident voice in his head telling him he was never quite good enough.

He didn't want to lose her but he didn't see what other choice he had. Since the day he found out she was pregnant with his child, his one goal in life had been to convince her they should marry. He had done everything in his power to convince her. Now he could only be profoundly grateful for her stubbornness in continuing to refuse.

He still believed it was the decent, honorable thing to do. Intellectually he knew he should continue to press until she changed her mind. He wanted his child to have an intact home, a father and mother.

But he couldn't imagine any hell more exquisitely

painful than being married to Katie when she didn't love him.

He would be miserable. What's more, he would no doubt make her miserable, as well.

What was he supposed to do? A man had an obligation to take care of his child. He believed that with all his heart. But how could he sentence himself to a loveless marriage when he wanted so much more?

"The baby's fine, then?" Katie asked Laura two days after her mother's phone call.

"As far as I can tell." The doctor smiled and returned her stethoscope to the weatherproof backpack full of medical supplies she had brought with her for the visit to Sweetwater.

"The heartbeat is strong and healthy," Laura went on, "and the baby's growth seems right on target for fourteen weeks. I've said it before, there are no guarantees when it comes to babies. But I've learned to trust my gut on these matters, and all my instincts are telling me you're past the danger zone of losing the pregnancy."

Katie let out the breath she'd been holding. Relief flooded through her like spring runoff, washing away the fear and worry she had carried around since the day of her fall. She wanted to hold her baby in her arms and whirl around the room.

Instead she contented herself with giving Laura a radiant smile. "Oh, thank you!"

Laura laughed. "Don't thank me. I didn't do anything. You're the one doing all the hard work here."

"I haven't done anything but lie around."

"That's just what you needed to be doing. Enjoy this chance to rest while you have it because once your little kiddo enters the picture, you'll forget you ever once had such a luxury as leisure time."

Laura's smile included Peter, sitting quietly in the armchair by the fireplace. "When do Clint and Margie return?" she asked.

"They called about an hour ago and said they should be here first thing in the morning," Katie said. "Their daughter caught the flu right after the delivery so they stayed until she was back on her feet."

"It's a good thing you had Mr. Logan here to help out while they were gone."

Katie managed a smile while inside some of her bleak mood returned. Peter *had* been a lifesaver, she admitted. But in the two day since Sheila called, things between them had changed.

He still cared for her just as diligently as before. He still cooked for her and took care of the animals and watched over her. He still talked to her and read to her and watched old movies with her, but all with a new reserve between them.

He wasn't cold exactly, simply stiff and withdrawn, as if trying to maintain a safe distance between them.

For two days he had been kind and solicitous but

all with that same polite detachment. And he hadn't said a single word in all that time about marriage.

Though she mourned his change of heart, she understood it and couldn't fault him for it.

He had only heard her part of the conversation with Sheila and missed out on most of the anti-Logan vitriol her mother had spewed. Nevertheless Katie was sure the one-sided snippets were enough to remind him of all the reasons they could never make a successful marriage.

She had seen the sudden panic flare in his eyes before he rushed outside on the flimsy excuse of taking care of livestock that certainly didn't need caring for.

She had known even then that he had changed his mind about marrying her. She tried to convince herself she was glad. Things surely would be easier between them if he dropped the ridiculous idea.

Wasn't she a contrary thing, though? Now that he stopped asking her, she could think of nothing she wanted more than to say yes.

"As far as I'm concerned," Laura went on, "you're cleared to return to Portland whenever you decide you're ready. Check in with your own obstetrician as soon as you get back. I'm sure she'll want to see you as soon as possible. But if you were my patient, I wouldn't put you on any other restrictions besides exercising normal caution. You're free to resume all your regular activities."

Oh, she didn't want to return to Portland and all

the chaos that awaited her there. She dreaded facing her family with the news of her pregnancy. Her siblings would have mixed feelings about the baby, she knew. Ivy would be thrilled their babies would be born only months apart and Trent knew she longed for a child. But she knew both of them would worry about her having the child on her own.

Jack would probably show her his typical distracted indifference. And Sheila... Well, Sheila would go ballistic, especially when she learned who the father was, something Katie realized now she couldn't hide.

Her mother had called a half-dozen times since their conversation two days earlier but Katie chose not to answer when she saw the number flashing on the caller ID.

She just didn't think she was up to a confrontation with her mother yet, but she knew she couldn't put it off much longer.

She pushed away her dread to deal with later. For now she would focus on her overwhelming joy that all appeared to be well with her baby.

She squeezed Laura's hand. "Thank you for everything."

"You can thank me by letting me hold a bouncing, healthy baby in a few months."

"It's a deal." Katie smiled.

Laura kissed her cheek, then shrugged into her heavy parka. Before she could pick up her bulky pack, Peter beat her to it.

"Let me carry this out to your vehicle for you."

"I never turn down a handsome man." Laura winked at Katie, kissed her again and followed Peter outside.

She would love to have Laura deliver her baby, she thought as she watched them go out into the pale twilight. Not only was she a dear friend but Katie trusted her medical skills implicitly. If Laura didn't love the rural Wyoming lifestyle where she had raised her own family, she could have been practicing medicine anywhere in the world.

Could she manage it somehow? Katie wondered. Maybe Laura would consent to fly out to Portland for the birth or Katie could always return to Sweetwater and have the baby here. Laura's clinic wasn't set up for childbirth but perhaps they could go to the small hospital in Jackson Hole.

The idea appealed deeply and she vowed to talk it over with Peter. Whether he wanted to marry her or not, he had a say in all of this, she admitted to herself.

A few moments later Peter returned to the great room, his expression remote, as it had been since her mother's phone call. "If you're ready to go back to Portland, we can fly out together after the Taylors return in the morning."

She sighed, hating this distance between them. "I suppose I have to. If I don't return soon, Trent will come and yank me back."

His mouth tightened as if he disliked the mention of her brother. "I hope you're not planning to jump right back into the deep end. Despite Dr. Harp's ringing endorsement that everything should be fine, I think you need to take it easy now."

She raised an eyebrow at his dictatorial tone. "I have a job to do, a career I enjoy that I'm good at."

"I'm sure you do. But I know damn well how stressful R & D can be. The long hours at a computer, the constant pressure to come up with something new. I'm just suggesting you think about whether that's really the best environment for a pregnant woman. You have a baby to think about now."

In the last few days her abdomen had seemed to swell rapidly, as if the baby decided there was no reason to hide her presence anymore. Katie loved her new roundness, loved seeing the little mound and imagining the person inside.

"Believe me," she retorted, "I'm very well aware of that fact, Peter. But I'm not one of your employees that you can order around. You're not my boss or my husband or my father."

Before her mother's phone call, he probably would have come back with something about how he wanted to be her husband; she only had to say the word.

Instead his mouth tightened. "But I am the father of that child you're carrying. Whether you like it or not, that gives me certain responsibilities to make sure you don't wear yourself out during the pregnancy with unnecessary stress."

This concern was for his child, not for her. The

knowledge made her heart ache, made her tone more combative than she intended. "Are you planning to monitor my time card?" she snapped.

His tone was just as cold. "Will I have to?"

Oh, she wanted to weep at the distance between them. This autocratic stranger was so different from the teasing, smiling man she had come to know in the days since her accident—the man she had come to love. She wanted him back!

"I know my limits. I don't intend to exceed them," she said quietly. "Contrary to the way I seem to act around you, I'm not completely lacking in common sense."

"I never said anything about your common sense or lack thereof. But you have a taxing, stressful position. I know how things go on the corporate level. You think you're only going to work a little late to tie up some loose ends and before you know it, the clock tolls midnight and you have to be back for a 6:00 a.m. conference call with Tokyo."

She knew that only too well. She had grown up watching it firsthand with her father. Before she had been sent to boarding school, she remembered sometimes going weeks without seeing Jack. He invariably left before she rose, no matter how early she set her alarm, and he returned home long after she went to bed.

She had to hope Peter would be different, for her baby's sake.

"It doesn't have to be that way. You said the other day you have good people who work for you. So do I. I fully intend to cede some of my duties to them during the pregnancy and talk to Trent about cutting both my hours and my responsibilities after the baby arrives."

"I'm sure he'll be just thrilled about that." Peter's voice dripped with sarcasm.

"He'll deal with it."

"You seem remarkably certain of that."

"He's my brother and he loves me."

His skeptical look made her ache again for all that lay between them. "He does," she said sharply. "Believe it or not, even we Crosbys are capable of loving each other."

"I never said you weren't."

You didn't have to say it, she started to say, but before she could open her mouth to utter her hot words, the strangest sensation tickled inside her—a flutter in her womb, like the tiny touch of butterfly wings whispering together.

She thought maybe she imagined it but then she felt it again, stronger this time, unmistakable.

The baby!

She froze and one hand flew to her mouth while the other covered the swell of her abdomen.

This was real!

She had a little life growing inside her, someone whose arms or legs—or both!—were flailing around right this minute. An incredible rush of emotion poured through her—shock and excitement and joy—and she couldn't hold back her tears.

"What is it?" Peter's voice was urgent, his brown eyes shadowed with concern. "Are you cramping again? Do I need to call Dr. Harp back?"

"No." The sound was halfway between a laugh and a sob. "I just felt the baby move."

He stared at her, thunderstruck. "Are you sure?"

"Yes. Absolutely." Those tiny butterfly wings quivered once more and Katie laughed out loud. "There she goes again."

He still looked shell-shocked. "Isn't it too early for that?"

"The books I've read say the fetus starts moving independently at around seven weeks but the first time the mother can detect it is usually between thirteen and eighteen weeks. I'm on the early side of that spread, I suppose. Maybe she's going to be a soccer player."

"Do you think—" He paused and cleared gruffness from his throat. "Could I feel it?"

"I don't know. It's very light, just a flicker really. But you could try," she offered.

She felt suddenly shy when he crossed the room to her but she hitched up her shirt. He placed one of those warm, strong hands on her abdomen and Katie was overwhelmed at the intimacy of standing here with him, sharing the sweetness of the moment.

"Is he moving?" Peter asked.

"A little. Not as much as before. She must be tired out. Can you feel anything."

He shook his head but seemed reluctant to remove his hand. Katie didn't mind. Even though he was only touching her abdomen, she felt embraced by him, almost cherished. Her heart brimmed over with love for him and for their child, and she tried fiercely to burn this moment into her memory.

"We spent one night together and now there's a little life in there." His voice was low, gruff and tugged at her heart. "It's amazing."

"I know. It's the most incredible thing that's ever happened to me."

He curled his hand over her abdomen as if he couldn't bear to let go and she leaned into his solid strength. She didn't want to move, didn't want to shatter this fragile, wonderful peace.

"I know this baby wasn't something you wanted," she said after a moment.

"It was unexpected, certainly, but not unwanted."

If she hadn't already been deeply in love with him at that moment, the sincerity of his words would have done the trick.

Peter seemed as reluctant as she to sever this fragile connection between them. With his hand still warm on her skin, he moved to the plump sofa and pulled her onto his lap.

This wasn't bad, either, she decided. Not bad at all. She added another memory to her precious store.

"When I was about seven my father came home with a puppy," he said once they were settled. "Keep in mind, I had never said a word about getting one and had never even acknowledged to myself that I might like a pet until Dad showed up with the thing. From the moment I saw the little mutt, I adored him. Roscoe slept in my room until I went to college."

His words touched her, at the same time she grieved for a little boy she sensed had never felt completely secure in his parents' love.

"We're having a baby, not a puppy," she pointed out. "I wouldn't expect her to lick your hand or chew your slippers, at least not at first."

His laugh jostled her a little against his hard chest. "I know they're vastly different things but the principle's the same. I never knew how much I wanted a puppy until Dad brought Roscoe home."

He met her gaze with a tenderness in his eyes that stunned her. "And I never realized how much I wanted a child until I found out you were pregnant."

The tears burning behind her eyelids spilled out at his words. She sniffled, more in love with him than she ever believed possible.

At her tears, raw panic flickered across his features and his arms tightened around her. "Don't cry, Katie. Whatever I said, I'm sorry."

"It's the hormones," she lied, then decided she was tired of untruths between them. "Well, some of it's the hormones," she admitted. "Mostly I'm just so happy you want this baby as much as I do."

He was quiet for a long moment, an odd expression on his face. "Katie, I have to tell you something."

His voice sounded tight, almost nervous, and she suddenly didn't want to hear what he had to say. Whatever it was, it had to be something grim with that solemn look in his eyes.

"Later," she said. "Would you mind just kissing me for now?"

She didn't give him a chance to say no before she pressed her mouth to his.

He froze for one shocked second, his eyes wide, then he closed them and kissed her back with all the passion and heat that had been simmering between them for a week.

She didn't have the courage to tell him of her feelings but she could show him this way. Her arms held him close, her fingers entwining in his hair, as she poured into the kiss all the love she ached to give him.

They had kissed several times since he arrived at Sweetwater but every touch had been tarnished by the anger and tension simmering between them. For the first time since the night of the bachelor auction, she kissed him without reserve.

He groaned her name and pulled her closer, so close she could feel his erection jut against her hip. "You feel so good I could stay right here forever and do this."

"Okay," she murmured against his mouth. "But I think in three or four days we'd probably get hungry."

"By then the Taylors will be back. We can swallow mouthfuls of Margie's delicious stew between kisses."

Her laugh turned into a moan as he trailed kisses down her throat. All she could think about were Laura's parting words, that she didn't need to restrict normal activities.

Did that mean they could they make love? she wondered, blood pulsing thickly through her veins. She wanted to, desperately. Her body cried out for his touch, for the heat and wonder they had found together for only that one night.

His mouth touched the high slope of one aching, sensitive breast through the open neck of her shirt and she gasped.

She couldn't bear it. She wanted him to touch her completely, to bare her skin and draw a taut, achy nipple into his mouth.

"I should stop," he murmured.

"Why?"

"Because if I keep torturing myself like this, I won't be *able* to stop."

"I don't want you to."

He groaned and his mouth found hers again in a kiss that scorched her clear to her toes.

Somewhere in the middle of another of those long, drugging kisses, she was vaguely aware of a noise that didn't belong, the squeak of the front door opening.

Before she could force her numbed brain cells to work so she could figure out how to extricate herself from his arms and see why the door would be opening, she heard a terrible sound.

A truly awful sound.

The most hideous sound she could imagine under the circumstances.

"What the hell is going on here?"

Her mother's voice rang through the room like metal grating on metal.

Twelve

Katie scrambled to her feet, terribly conscious of her tousled, just-been-kissed disarray. She was vaguely aware of Peter rising, as well, smoothing down the shirt her hands must have rearranged.

Oh, this was horrible!

"M-mother. This is a surprise. What are you doing here?"

Sheila's collagen-implanted lips curled into a snarl. "What is *he* doing here? This is the *friend* staying in this hellhole with you? Peter Logan?" Her voice rose on the last word until she was nearly screeching.

"Yes."

"Quite the cozy little love nest you have here. No wonder you wouldn't tell me the name of your mystery man."

Katie blew out a breath. "I knew you wouldn't be pleased."

Sheila's face started turning so purple her makeup took on a garish hue. "Not pleased? Not *pleased?* Have you completely lost your mind? I knew you were up to something—you've always been a terrible liar—so I decided to stop here on my way back to Portland. In my wildest dreams I never would have expected this!"

Sheila flung each word at her like wickedly sharp rocks, and Katie couldn't help flinching.

"What were you thinking? He's a *Logan.*" She said the word like the most vulgar of obscenities. "Or at least one of the adopted ones."

Peter's features had been without expression since Sheila barged into the house, but at this, his jaw clenched and his eyes darkened with anger. He stepped forward but Katie put a hand on his arm, begging him silently to let her handle it.

If he entered the fray, Sheila would annihilate him. She fought dirty and had no compunction about kicking below the belt.

"Mother, I can explain," Katie said lamely.

"I certainly hope so." Sheila stalked in and plopped onto the chair opposite the couch where they stood.

Katie didn't know where to start. She didn't want

to tell her mother anything, not about the night of the gala and not about the days since. Somehow telling her mother would taint what had been the most wonderful time of her life.

Before she could catch hold of any of her wildly scrambling thoughts in order to offer some kind of coherent defense, Sheila's gaze landed on the stack of books on the coffee table between them.

"What is *this?*" She grabbed one and thrust it at Katie. *"Your Baby's First Nine Months?"*

She cringed. Oh, this was a nightmare. Worse than a nightmare. Katie closed her eyes, wishing she could retreat into her safe, invisible comfort zone. It was too late for that. She had walked out of that comfort zone forever the moment she let Carrie Summers talk her into a makeover.

"You want to tell me why you're reading pregnancy books?"

She opened her eyes and met her mother's gaze squarely. She refused to feel ashamed about her baby and she would do anything necessary to protect and defend this child. "The usual reason."

"You're *pregnant?*"

"Yes. About fourteen weeks along."

She had never seen her mother speechless but Sheila gaped for a full thirty seconds. All too soon, she found her voice. "He's the father? You got knocked up by Peter Logan?"

"This is not some version of *Rosemary's Baby*,

Mother. He's not the devil incarnate." She wasn't sure where the sarcasm came from but it was too late to stow it back down.

"He might as well be!"

Sheila looked her up and down with more than her usual distaste and Katie burned under the perusal. "What were you thinking, Katherine? Are you truly that desperate for a man in your bed that you'll even sleep with a Logan?"

Though she wanted to stay calm and in control, Katie swayed a little from the attack. She brushed against Peter's chest and for the first time realized he was standing at her back.

At Sheila's words, though, he stepped forward, his eyes blazing. "That's enough," he snapped.

"I wondered if you were going to say anything or just stand there, you bastard. We both know damn well a man like you could never be attracted to Katie. What were you after, then? Crosby company secrets? Did she tell you any? I hope they were worth all you must have had to go through to get them."

Katie wanted to die. She wanted to curl up into a ball of humiliation and expire on the spot. The really sad thing was, she could have written the script for this conversation with her mother almost word for word, right down to Sheila's disbelief that someone like Peter Logan would ever be genuinely interested in her.

"Why not?" Peter asked.

Sheila looked baffled by his question. "What?"

"Why wouldn't I be attracted to Katie?"

Sheila arched one of her carefully waxed eyebrows. "I've seen the women you date. Katherine couldn't even be a bat girl in your league. She wears baggy clothes and she never does a thing with her makeup. She'd rather have her nose stuck in a book than have her nails done, and she wouldn't be able to tell a Dior from a Wang if her life depended on it. I love my daughter, Mr. Logan, but you have to admit, she's a mess."

Peter stared at her for several long moments, then shook his head, utter contempt in his eyes. "You are one first-rate bitch."

Sheila sputtered as if no one had ever called her that before, but Peter ignored her.

"Have you ever even looked at your daughter?" he asked.

"Of course I've looked at her. She's come a long way since college when she was fat and had hair like Cousin Itt. But she's not one of your slinky supermodels and she never will be."

Never in his life had he come so close to belting a woman. It was all he could do to keep his hands clenched at his sides, especially when he saw how pale Katie was.

Her hands were trembling and she looked mortified to have them fighting over her like this. He wanted to gather her close and kiss away all the pain he saw in her eyes.

He couldn't believe any mother would be so cruel to her own child. Mothers were supposed to think their children were the most beautiful creations on the planet. They were supposed to do anything they could to defend them from attacks like this one, not be the one doing the attacking.

How could Sheila be so blind about her daughter's loveliness?

Or was she?

Maybe she saw it clearly enough to feel threatened by it. The idea made sense. He had a feeling Sheila Crosby was just the kind of woman who would grind anybody she viewed as competition under the heels of her four-inch stilettos, even her own daughter.

"You're right, she'll never be a supermodel. She's too short." He smiled at Katie who gazed back at him with wide, confused eyes. "But with a few more inches, she could walk any runway in the world."

He laughed as Katie visibly shuddered at the image. He loved this woman. Loved her fiercely.

He turned back to Sheila. "The first time I saw Katie, I thought she was the most stunning thing I had ever seen. Since I've come to know her better, I've come to realize the woman inside is even more beautiful than what she shows to the world."

Sheila narrowed her gaze at him as if trying to figure out what game he was playing. It never would have occurred to her that he could be sincere, he realized, despising her fiercely.

How could she have raised someone as sweet and loving as Katie? he wondered, until he remembered Katie said her brother had basically raised her and her siblings.

Maybe he needed to rethink his animosity toward Trent Crosby. He had done a damn good job with his sister.

"If you ever looked closely at your daughter the way I do," he went on, "you would see a beautiful, smart, courageous woman any mother should be proud of."

He leaned forward until Sheila could look nowhere but at him. "If you ever really saw Kate through anything other than your own middle-aged narcissism and envy at anyone younger and prettier than you, you would also see a woman who could have any man she wants. For some incredible reason, she wanted me and that makes me the luckiest damn idiot in the world."

Sheila's features filled with a deep rage that aged her at least a dozen years. "Get out," she snarled.

During his little speech Katie hadn't taken her gaze from him. She looked stunned, so awed by his words that he wanted fiercely to kiss her. Wouldn't Sheila just love that?

Katie seemed to collect herself and turned back to Sheila. "Sweetwater isn't part of your divorce settlement, Mother. You can't order anybody around here."

"Then you kick him out! See if you can get that

brain you're so damn proud of to work for five seconds and realize he's just using you to hurt Crosby Systems and the Crosby family."

"No. He's the father of my baby and he's asked me to marry him. I—I've decided I will."

She didn't look at him when she made her declaration—a good thing, he supposed, since he was sure someone had just shoved a bowling ball into his stomach.

"You're going to *marry* him?" Sheila looked as if she would spontaneously combust any second now.

Katie continued, "If he still wants me after he sees what kind of in-laws he'll be taking on."

Somehow Peter found his .voice, though it sounded as if he'd swallowed a cubic yard of gravel. "He does."

She finally met his gaze, and the tentative smile in her eyes had him tumbling hard for her all over again.

"You've gone absolutely mental," Sheila shrieked. "Wait until the rest of the family hears about this. They're going to go through the roof!"

"No, they won't."

Katie blinked as a sweet assurance settled in her heart. She had been so worried about her family's reaction at learning of her pregnancy but she suddenly realized as she listened to her mother rant that Sheila was the only one in the family who would be angry.

A huge weight lifted from her shoulders and she suddenly couldn't wait to tell the world about the baby.

"Trent and Ivy will be thrilled for me. Danny will be, too. They love me and want the best for me, regardless of some silly feud we had nothing to do with. When they realize this is what I want, they'll accept it. Jack might bluster a little but I'm sure Toni will eventually make him come around."

"I never will!" her mother snarled. "You can be sure of that! If you marry this…bastard, to me you'll be one of them and so will the brat you're knocked up with."

"If I were you, I would choose my next words very carefully." Peter's voice was tungsten-hard, the threat unmistakable. As usual, Sheila didn't heed the warning signs.

"You're not me," she snapped. "You're a *Logan*. A filthy, lying, son-of-a-bitch Logan!"

"Stop right there." Katie stepped forward, her face hot from shame and embarrassment. "I'm sorry you feel that way. If you can't accept my child and be civil to Peter and his family, then I suppose we have nothing more to say to each other."

Her mother had never physically struck her but somehow Katie sensed that if Peter hadn't been standing beside her, she would have felt the sting of her mother's hand for the first time in her life. Instead Sheila stared at her for a long moment, then stomped out of the house, slamming the door so hard the windows quivered.

As soon as her mother left, Katie wanted to sink

through the floor and disappear. Maybe if she were lucky, the force of that slamming door would collapse the roof in the next ten seconds, burying her in eight feet of snow so she wouldn't have to face Peter.

She had to settle for burying her face in her hands. "I'm so sorry," she murmured. "I'm afraid Sheila can be a little, um, difficult."

His laugh held deep amusement at her understatement. "I guess you could say that."

"I don't blame you for changing your mind about wanting to marry me, Peter. No matter what you said to my mother, you don't have to go through with it."

"I never changed my mind."

"Then why haven't you said a word about it for the last few days?"

He said nothing for so long she finally dropped her hands and squared her shoulders to face him. His mouth was tight and his eyes were dark with an unreadable expression, something deep and tender that sent butterflies somersaulting around her stomach.

"I meant what I said to your mother. I think you're a beautiful, smart, courageous woman. I didn't tell her everything, though."

He reached between them to clasp her fingers. The butterflies went into cartwheels and handsprings as her heart began to pump.

"No?" her voice sounded like a mouse's tiny squeak but he didn't appear to notice.

Peter shook his head. "I didn't tell her that night

we spent together was the most incredible, magical night of my life. I didn't tell her how I searched for you for weeks and how empty and lonely my life seemed from the moment I woke alone in my bed until I found you again."

He was quiet again, then his gaze met hers. "I didn't tell her I fell in love that night."

For one brief moment, a brilliant, piercing joy washed through her, then she realized what he said and the joy quickly turned to ashes. "You fell in love with an illusion. Celeste wasn't real."

"She's part of you, whether you can see it or not."

Katie made a skeptical sound and Peter raised their entwined fingers and kissed the back of her hand. "She is. You're right, though, maybe I didn't know the real you after that single incredible night. But we've had more than that here and I've only fallen more deeply in love with you every day we've been together."

His kiss was sweet and tender and warmed all the cold, empty places inside of her. She clung to him, tears trickling down her cheeks.

"Blasted hormones," she mumbled through her tears. She had cried more the last week than she had her entire adult life.

"I hope those are happy tears," Peter murmured.

"They are. Oh, they are."

She kissed him with all the love and longing she had been saving for years. When he drew away several moments later, both of them were breathing raggedly and Peter's eyes were dazed, aroused.

He said only one word. "Wow."

She laughed even though those dratted tears continued to fall. He gently wiped one away with his thumb before it reached her cheek, then shook his head as if to clear it.

"I told your mother you could have your pick of any man in the world. Why did you pick me that night? I figured out a long time ago you weren't after Logan secrets. Why did you come home with me?"

Was that insecurity in his eyes? she wondered. Could he really not know how irresistible he was?

"You don't remember the first time we danced, do you? Not the night of the gala but long before then."

He shook his head, baffled.

"I do. Every second of it. I was fifteen years old and fat. Not chubby, fat. Sheila dressed me in ruffles and bows for my first big society event during one of my visits home and I looked hideous, with thick glasses and all those flounces."

She grimaced at the memory. "I felt even more miserable than I'm sure I looked. I didn't want to be there. I wanted to be home with a good book. Even boarding school would have been better."

Though he was confused, he didn't interrupt her story, curious where this was all going.

"I was an easy target for several girls who—who liked to pick on anyone more vulnerable than they were. We were standing in a corner of the ballroom and they started making fun of me, saying I looked like a giant pink birthday cake with all my flounces, which was nothing but the truth. I was trying my best not to let them see me cry but I was losing the battle. Then you came over."

He should remember. He *wanted* to remember but he'd been to so many of those kinds of functions, and this one just didn't stand out.

"You were eighteen and heading to college and all the girls were crazy about you."

She smiled a little. "You probably didn't know that, did you? As I remember, you were busy even then trying to follow in your father's footsteps. Anyway, Angelina Mitchell was the prettiest of the group and she preened a little, certain, I'm sure, that you were going to ask her to dance. But you didn't. You walked right up to me—shy, fat Katie Crosby!—and asked me in this deep, confident voice if I would do you the great honor of dancing with you."

He could feel himself flush, though he wasn't sure why. He still couldn't remember the event, maybe because he had often danced with wallflowers at country club functions or other society events. He had never had much interest in the popular girls. At least the wallflowers usually made halfway decent conversation and wanted to know more about him than what kind of car he drove.

He cleared the sudden gruffness from his voice. "I guess we danced, then?"

She nodded and he felt about a hundred miles tall at the stars in her eyes at the memory. "I know you were only being kind, rescuing me from what you must have figured out was the other girls' bullying, but it was the most romantic moment of my life. I think I fell in love with you that night."

His arms tightened around her and he closed his eyes, supremely grateful for a mother who drilled kindness and good manners into her sons.

"I haven't felt beautiful very often in my life," Katie went on. "That was the first time. The second time was the night of the charity gala. When you danced with me, I was fifteen years old again, in the arms of the most wonderful boy I'd ever met. I didn't want it to end. That's why I didn't tell you my name, because I wanted that night to last forever."

He shifted his hand to the swelling of her abdomen, to their child growing there. "In a way, I guess it has."

Her smile was radiant as she kissed him again. "That was the perfect thing to say," she murmured. "This baby is a gift. A precious way to help us always remember a wonderful, magical night. I love you, Peter. I loved you when I was fifteen and I love you a million times more now."

"When will you marry me?" he asked, when he could speak again through the emotions clogging his throat.

Doubts flickered in her eyes again. "Are you sure? You saw tonight what you might be in for. And what about your parents? They won't be thrilled about all this."

"When they get to know you, they'll love you as much as I do." It was true, he realized. His mom and Katie would bond instantly. His father might be a little harder to win over but he would be impressed by her brains and her business sense. Affection would soon follow. Terrence wouldn't be able to resist her.

"Marry me, Katie," he urged, his hand still on her abdomen. "Right now. Tonight. We can fly to Las Vegas and be married by midnight. I don't want to waste another moment."

She drew in a deep breath, then covered her hand with his, until they were both cradling the child growing there.

"All right." She gave him another one of those radiant smiles. "Let's go now. We have a new family dynasty to create."

One that would be built on joy and laughter and love.

Epilogue

"You look beautiful, Katie. I don't have to ask if Logan is making you happy. If the power suddenly went out in here, you would give off enough of a glow to light up the whole place."

Katie smiled at Trent, handsome and commanding in his tuxedo. "I'm happier than I've ever been in my life."

"Good. You deserve it. And I guess if Peter Logan is the one making you so happy, he can't be all bad."

Trent's bluster was mostly for show, she knew. Her brother and her new husband had actually gotten along remarkably well after she and Peter returned from their brief honeymoon. The two men were alike in far more ways than they were different.

As she and Trent twirled around the Hilton ballroom—where it all began, she thought with a smile—Katie gazed around at the crowd that had gathered to celebrate her marriage to Peter. Hundreds of people were here. Leslie Logan had thrown herself with enthusiasm into organizing the reception. She had invited not only all the Logan and Crosby employees but also employees at Portland General Hospital and Children's Connection, until the big room was filled to bursting.

Even the *Portland Weekly* society reporter was there. Katie had made a special point of making sure he received an invitation, since without that picture she and Peter wouldn't have found each other again.

Everyone she loved was in this room, she thought. Except Danny, who hadn't been able to leave his island retreat.

Her father was dancing with Toni. Ivy, glowing from pregnancy herself, was in the arms of her handsome king.

To her surprise, Sheila had even come, though under duress. She still wasn't at all pleased about her daughter marrying a Logan. But after Jack had surprised Katie by threatening to take Sheila back to court to reduce her alimony if she didn't support her daughter, Sheila seemed to resign herself to it.

She was coldly polite to Peter, but that was more than Katie ever expected.

Like a magnet finding north, her eyes turned automatically to her husband, currently smiling down at Dorothea Aldridge as they whirled around the room together.

She turned back to her brother. "Peter is wonderful. Every day I fall more in love with him."

Trent sighed. "You know, I envy you. I wish my own trip down the aisle had turned out as well as yours."

She hugged him, her heart aching for him even in the midst of her bubbling joy. She knew how much the failure of his marriage stung him. "I know. I do, too. But maybe the Crosby luck is finally changing. Ivy and Max are deliriously happy, just as Peter and I are. We both found love—maybe you and Danny will have your turn soon."

Trent looked skeptical but before he could reply, Peter whirled Mrs. Aldridge toward them and tapped Trent on the shoulder.

"Dorothea says now that I'm no longer available, dancing with me isn't nearly as much fun as it used to be. She's got this thing for bachelors. Since I told her you're the most eligible one I know, she decided she didn't want to waste her time dancing with an old married man like me and insisted we trade partners."

"We Crosbys are better dancers anyway." Trent smiled at Dorothea, who chuckled and allowed herself to be handed off to him. The two of them spun away, leaving Peter to take Katie into his arms.

"Smooth. Very smooth, Mr. Logan," she mimicked her words of that night months before.

He played along. "When a beautiful woman crosses my path, I'm not stupid enough to give her any chance to slip away."

"This woman doesn't want to slip away," she murmured. "She doesn't want to be anywhere but right here, in your arms."

He kissed her, and though it was chaste enough for the family crowd gathered in the ballroom, her insides still clenched with desire. Every time they touched, this same heat sparked between them.

She had to admit she'd been a little afraid the wild passion between them after the charity gala had just been chance, a result of the romance of the night and maybe too much champagne. But any doubts she might have had on that score were quickly laid to rest on their honeymoon. She flushed, remembering.

If anything, their lovemaking had been better. Their shared love added a deep emotional intensity she never would have imagined.

She was warm suddenly from more than the exertion and the crowded ballroom. "I could use some water and fresh air."

With the solicitous care that constantly amazed her, he led her over to the bar and snagged a glass of ice water. "I'm sorry you can't have champagne," he said when he handed the water to her.

She made a wry face. "I'm not. It makes me do crazy things."

"I know. Believe me, I plan to keep that in mind after you have the baby."

His teasing leer made her laugh. "I don't need champagne when I'm around you. You're intoxicating enough."

At that, he had to stop and kiss her again. When he lifted his head, Katie felt someone watching them. She shifted her gaze from Peter's to find a dark-haired man watching them. He looked somehow familiar but she couldn't place him. She gave him a hesitant smile, a little unnerved by something in his expression.

He quickly looked away but not before she thought she saw confusion and naked pain in his eyes.

That was odd, she thought, but her attention was diverted when Leslie and Terrence approached them. Peter kissed his mother on the cheek while Terrence threaded his arm through Katie's

"Everything is so lovely," Katie told Peter's mother. "You did a wonderful job with this reception."

"It's not every day that a mother's oldest son gets married." Leslie smiled at her. "And since we missed that part when the two of you rushed to Las Vegas, I wanted the reception to be spectacular."

That had been one of the biggest shocks of her marriage, Katie acknowledged. Peter had been right. Once they learned a child was on the way and realized their son loved her, Terrence and Leslie had welcomed her into their family—with hesitant arms at first, but their initial reserve had quickly melted. Already she was coming to care for them.

"Thank you. We'll remember this night for the rest of our lives."

Leslie smiled and reached for her hand. "You make a beautiful bride, Katie. My son is a lucky man."

She still wasn't sure she quite believed that—the beautiful part anyway—but after a week of marriage, she was beginning to see herself through different eyes. Maybe it was pregnancy, or maybe it came from being so deeply loved, but she had decided she wasn't the Crosby ugly duckling after all. She never had been. She had just preferred hiding in that invisible comfort zone.

Leaving it had been terrifying but so worth it, Katie thought, a sweet joy settling in her chest. Who would have believed the night of the bachelor charity auction that in a few months' time she would find herself married to the man she had loved since an act of kindness more than a decade ago, the man she loved more than she ever thought possible?

The baby moved, almost as if sensing her thoughts, and she smiled and touched a hand to her abdomen.

"How's he doing?" Peter asked. An ultrasound the day before had revealed their child was definitely a boy.

"Fine. I think he wants to dance."

Peter smiled. "We'd better oblige him, don't you think?"

Their baby would come into a loving home, Katie thought as her husband took her into his arms, to a mother and father who already adored him and each other.

She couldn't ask for anything more.

With an odd feeling of unreality, Everett Baker watched the newly married couple share a tender embrace then turn to smile at the groom's parents.

The Logans' oldest son and his bride.

His chest tightened and he couldn't seem to breathe in the stuffy ballroom. He felt odd, dizzy and a little nauseated as he watched them together. They looked so in love, so full of joy.

He should never have come. He didn't belong here with these happy, good, decent people. But when that invitation had arrived, as it had to all employees of Children's Connection, he had stared at a single line for hours.

Peter Logan, son of Leslie and Terrence Logan.

The line rang in his head like some horrible nursery rhyme, crowding everything else out until it was the only thing he could think about.

He hadn't been able to stay away but now that he was here, he knew coming had been a terrible mistake.

You're nothing, boy. Less than nothing.

He heard Lester Baker's voice in his head, as he

did so often, and knew the man was right. Everett
shouldn't be here. He didn't *deserve* to be here.

He jostled his way through the crowd and hurried
out the door, away from all this laughter and dancing and painful happiness and into the darkness
where he belonged.

* * * * *

*Turn the page for a sneak preview
of the next emotional LOGAN'S LEGACY title,*
THE SECRET HEIR
*by reader favorite Gina Wilkins
on sale in February 2005...*

One

Laurel Phillips Reiss was a strong, competent, self-sufficient woman. Everyone who knew her said so. She could handle anything.

Anything except this.

Twisting a shredded tissue between her hands, she looked through her lashes at the man sitting in a nearby chair in the hospital waiting room. His sun-streaked blond hair was tousled from running his hands through it. Strong emotions darkened his blue eyes to navy and hardened his chiseled features to resemble granite. Years of manual labor had toned his broad-shouldered body. Jackson Reiss looked fit, tough and strong enough to overcome any adversity.

Except this one.

His eyes met hers. "Are you okay?"

She nodded, but even that silent response was a lie. She wasn't at all okay.

Other people sat in the waiting room, clustered in tight units as they waited for news of loved ones. Conversations swirled around them, the volume fluctuating from muted to rather loud. Occasional bursts of self-conscious, too-cheery laughter were followed by nervous silences. On the far side of the waiting room, a young woman cried softly. Laurel watched as a man gathered her into his arms to comfort her.

The green-upholstered chairs in which Laurel and Jackson sat were crowded together so that their knees almost touched, but they made no effort to close even that small distance. Laurel's hands were in her lap, and Jackson's were fisted on his knees. A plain gold band gleamed on the ring finger of her left hand. His hands were bare, since jewelry could be dangerous on the construction sites where he spent most of his time.

There might as well have been a wall between them.

A dark-haired man who looked maybe ten years older than Laurel's twenty-six approached them with a respectful, slightly weary expression. He wore a white lab coat over a blue shirt and khakis. His tie was a riot of color. A nametag identified him as "Michael Rutledge, M.D." "Mr. and Mrs. Reiss?"

Laurel surged to her feet as Jackson did the same.

"How is Tyler?" she asked urgently. "What's wrong with him?"

"If you'll both follow me." He motioned toward a row of doors at one end of the waiting room. "We can talk privately in a conference room."

Laurel felt a band tighten around her heart. If he wanted to talk to them in private, then something must really be wrong, she thought in despair. Wouldn't he have already reassured them if everything was fine?

Her body felt stiff and unresponsive when she tried to move. She stumbled a little, and Jackson reached out immediately to steady her. For only a moment, she allowed herself to sag against him, drawing on his strength. But then she squared her shoulders and stepped away from him. "I'm all right," she murmured.

Her husband nodded and shoved his hands into the pockets of the faded jeans he wore with battered work boots and a denim shirt. Dressed more colorfully in a red jacket and black slacks, Laurel moved a couple of steps ahead of Jackson as she followed the doctor into a small room with four straight-back chairs arranged around a round table.

A box of tissues sat on the table. A smudged dry-erase board hung on one wall, and a peaceful painting of mountains and clouds on another. A tall green plant stood in one corner; it needed water, Laurel noted automatically, focusing on inconsequential matters until she was certain she had her emotions under tight control.

"Please, Mrs. Reiss." Dr. Rutledge held a chair for her. "Sit down."

She would rather have stood, but she sank onto the edge of the chair. Jackson took the seat beside her—close, but again, without touching her. Both Laurel and Jackson kept their eyes on the doctor as he took a chair across from them. Laurel started to speak, but discovered that her throat was too tight. Hearing Jackson draw a deep breath, she let him ask the question that was paramount to both of them.

"What's wrong with our son?"

Before the doctor could reply, a fortysomething woman with fiery red hair, a round, freckled face, and a plumply maternal figure knocked once and entered the room, carrying a thick file. "Sorry," she murmured to the doctor. "I got delayed."

"No problem." Dr. Rutledge stood upon the nurse's entrance. "Mr. and Mrs. Reiss, this is Kathleen O'Hara, the nurse practitioner who has been assigned to Tyler. She'll be your contact person who can answer all your questions during Tyler's treatment."

Nodding perfunctorily to the nurse, Jackson waited only until they were seated before saying again, "What's wrong with our son?"

Laurel tried to concentrate on the rather technical information the doctor gave them for the next ten minutes or so, but the words seemed to fly past her in a haze. She absorbed just enough to understand that her precious three-year-old son was suffering from a potentially fatal heart valve defect.

"The good news is that we've caught the condition early," Dr. Rutledge assured them, leaning slightly toward Laurel as he spoke. "All too often, the first sign of trouble is when a young person with this defect—usually a male in his late teens or early twenties—drops dead after participating in a rigorous sport. That's not going to happen with Tyler because we know what we're dealing with."

"You said he'll need a couple of operations. One now, and one more as he grows." Jackson's voice was rather hoarse. Glancing his way, Laurel saw that the sun lines around his eyes and mouth had deepened, and that much of the color had drained from his tanned face. "How dangerous are those operations?"

"I won't lie to you. There's always a risk during surgery." The surgeon spent another few minutes outlining the possible complications, what Laurel had always thought of as the medical "C.Y.A." spiel. He spoke with practiced compassion, a speech he had obviously made many times before.

Laurel had to make an effort to sit still and listen quietly when every maternal cell within her was urging her to run screaming to Tyler's side, where she could gather him into her arms and protect him from

harm. This wasn't just any sick child Michael Rutledge was discussing in such bewilderingly complex
terms. This was Laurel's baby. The one perfect part
of her life.

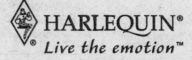

LOGAN'S LEGACY

Because birthright has its privileges and family ties run deep.

Silhouette Books invites you to come back and visit the Logan family!

Just collect six (6) proofs of purchase from the back of six (6) different LOGAN'S LEGACY titles and receive FOUR free LOGAN'S LEGACY books that are not not currently available in retail outlets!

Just complete the order form and send it, along with six (6) proofs of purchase from six (6) different LOGAN'S LEGACY titles to: LOGAN'S LEGACY, P.O. Box 9047, Buffalo, NY 14269-9047, or P.O. Box 613, Fort Erie, Ontario L2A 5X3.
(No cost for shipping and handling)

Name (PLEASE PRINT)

Address   Apt. #

City   State/Prov.   Zip/Postal Code

                                                                093 KJY DXH6

When you return six proofs of purchase, you will receive the following titles:

THE GREATEST RISK by Cara Colter
WHAT A MAN NEEDS by Patricia Thayer
UNDERCOVER PASSION by Raye Morgan
ROYAL SEDUCTION by Donna Clayton

Remember—to receive all four (4) titles, you must send six (6) original proofs of purchase. (Please allow 4-8 weeks for delivery. Offer expires August 31, 2005. Offer available in Canada and the U.S. only.)

When you respond to this offer, we will also send you *Inside Romance*, a free quarterly publication, highlighting upcoming releases and promotions from Harlequin and Silhouette Books.

☐ If you do not wish to receive this free publication, please check here.

Silhouette®
Where love comes alive™

LOGAN'S LEGACY

Because birthright has its privileges and family ties run deep.

ONE PROOF OF PURCHASE
LLPOP8

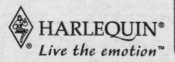

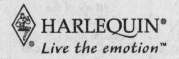

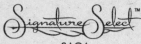

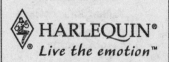

SPECIAL EDITION™

Discover why readers love
Sherryl Woods!

THE ROSE COTTAGE SISTERS

Love and laughter surprise them at their childhood haven.

THREE DOWN THE AISLE

by Sherryl Woods

Stunned when a romance blows up in her face, Melanie D'Angelo reluctantly takes refuge in her grandmother's cottage on the shores of Chesapeake Bay. But when local landscaper Mike Mikelewski arrives with his daughter to fix her grandmother's garden, suddenly Melanie's heart is on the mend as well!

**Silhouette Special Edition #1663
On sale February 2005!**

Meet more Rose Cottage Sisters later this year!

WHAT'S COOKING—Available April 2005
THE LAWS OF ATTRACTION—Available May 2005
FOR THE LOVE OF PETE—Available June 2005

Only from Silhouette Books!

Where love comes alive™